Inner Passion

Sexy
Stories
Collection

VOLUME 18

14 EROTIC SHORT STORIES

STEFAN MCKINNIS

Inner Passion/ Stefan McKinnis. -- 1st ed.
Xplicit Press, an imprint of TLM Media LLC

ISBN-13: 978-1-62327-549-5
ISBN-10: 1-62327-549-0
eISBN 978-1-62327-599-0

Printed in the United States of America

CONTENTS

1 THE SPICE OF MARRIAGE

A Frustrated Wife

Lori waited impatiently in bed. The anticipation of seeing her husband come out naked still got her heart rate up. Even in middle age, Roger was a good-looking man. Despite two kids and 15 years of marriage, the idea of him penetrating her with that exciting erection never failed to get her aroused.

Roger came out of the bathroom towelling his naked body off. That beautiful cock was swaying between his legs but not erect. "Hi big boy," Lori cooed. "Do you want this?" At that, she opened her legs to let him get a good view of her pussy just under her shortie nightgown. She was pleased that he stared, but he did not get hard about it like he did when they were wild sexual animals.

"You can fuck me all night tiger," Lori

moaned, hoping a little dirty talk would do the trick. He did smile at hearing the Sunday school teacher mom talk like a prostitute. Most guys would be able to put an eye out with their erection if a woman said that to him. But 15 years of sex took its toll. The sizzle was almost gone from their sex life.

Lori still had her needs and there was only so much she could do with her fingers and a glass of wine. She did not want to get a vibrator, a lover, or read porn to get off. She wanted the man who used to make her almost pass out from orgasms do it to her that hard and ferocious again. That is what being married meant. She just had to find a way to turn him back into the crazed sex maniac for her he used to be.

"Be right there, Hun," he said without feeling. She might have been offering him a BLT sandwich the way he responded instead of the chance to fuck her brains out. Maybe it was the nightie. Maybe she should shave so her pussy looked like a twelve year old. Maybe role-play. Lori was about ready to try anything.

Roger finally climbed into bed and turned out the light. He was kissing her neck, so this showed promise. Lori slid her hand down and wrapped it around his long cock. But it was not fully erect yet. "I want you to fuck me like the slut that I am," she moaned into his ear. She felt him begin to get stiff. But it was not the rock hard stallion cock she used to know.

It was enough. She slipped it into her

vagina rim and pressed up so it entered her. She moaned happily. "Make me cum babe," she whispered, biting his ear. He began to fuck her immediately, but it was mechanical. She suspected he was thinking of someone else. He did not play with her tits or squeeze her ass. Lori kept up the pressure to make it an erotic fuck. But she was doing all the work. She even had to thrust up to meet his fucking motions because the enthusiasm was not there.

When Roger shot, it was a weak stream. He rolled off and Lori was left without her orgasm again. She laid there as he almost immediately started to snore. Lori got up and went to the other bathroom so he would not wake up and see that she was not with him. The kids, Betsy 7 and Jordon 9, were fast asleep in their rooms and they slept like the dead. So she could use their big bathroom and that big tub in there to relax.

She locked the door and looked in the mirror. She was still a beautiful woman and she knew that because she saw men at the market, at school functions, or at church check her out. Cyndi, her best friend, described her as a young Annette Benning, but that could be a stretch. Still she was quite desirable if only it was Roger who would desire her.

Lori drew a hot bath and eased her naked body into it. She began to remember the passionate Roger who could hardly be contained from fucking her many times a day. She complained of being sore from how often he bent her over and buried that rock hard cock into her anywhere in the house. As she remembered that exciting erotic man, she began to stroke her clitoris. She arched up and saw that pink nub of her clit stand up above the folds of her pussy. She massaged it and moaned feeling her own passion come to the surface.

Her finger drifted to her vagina rim to stroke it. She finally slipped a finger inside. Her mind was 20 years ago and her pussy was on fire for the man she adored. The water sloshed as she thrust up to meet the hard fucking he was giving her in her imagination. Suddenly her orgasm hit and she gasped and jerked back and then relaxed.

As she let the warm water take over, Lori began to feel sleepy. Just then, she heard the soft hum of her cell phone on the toilet seat where she put it. It was Cyndi. Always nice to talk to her dearest friend. Cyndi was amused that she was talking to Lori as she relaxed in the tub. They caught up on the day and then Lori confided in her friend her frustration with her sex life. This was not the first time Cyndi had heard it. Cyndi was 32, just a few years younger than Lori and she too had to take some drastic steps to put the fire back in the pants of her husband Steven.

"Lori you know what you are going to have to do, don't you?" Cyndi asked.

"Tell me. I am about at the end of my rope." Lori responded.

"You are going to have to do something dramatic and dangerous to get his attention. Make him notice the hot sex kitten you are.

Make a statement that hot hubby of yours cannot ignore."

Making a Statement

Cindy's advice sunk in and Lori took her time planning the seduction of Roger, her own husband. Her first step was to stop giving it away. The pleading sexually deprived wife in the bedroom started playing hard to get. This was just step one so Lori did not let it bother her when Roger barely noticed.

Friday rolled around and Roger and Lori had a date. They supported a local theatre group because relatives performed in the plays. The group was performing Our Town at the Civic Center, which was a big deal because they got to use a professional stage instead of their usual small amateur playhouse.

Lori planed this scheme down to the details. She wore a gorgeous yellow sundress for the warm summer night weather. She shaved her legs all the way up to her belly button. Above all, there were no panties under that skirt. That was for Roger and only Roger. That was the fun part of this plan.

Roger dropped Lori off and she went into the lobby as he parked the car. She found just the right spot so she would not be easy to find. Lori was giddy with anticipation and waited for him to become frantic. Just then, her cell phone rang and it was Roger.

"Where are you!" he demanded.

Lori whispered in the phone. "If you want me, find me. Up the hall, just inside the side door to the theatre."

There was a bench in there where the ushers could sit just a few yards away from that door. Lori was ready when Roger pulled open the door. She lifted her legs so her heels rested on the bench and her pussy was visible between her pressed together thighs. Roger came through and saw her giving him a private show of her freshly shaved pussy.

"Lori are you..." And he stopped in his tracks staring at the erotic display of his sexy wife. "Oh my God, Lori," was all he could say because just then she opened her legs wide so the wet folds of her cunt opened to him to come and get her. She smiled with victory as a huge bulge surged into his pants. Then she moaned to him low tones like a cat in heat.

"Come and take this, Tiger, or someone else will."

As Roger lunged forward, Lori stood up to be swept up in his embrace. The kiss that took over her lips was more passionate than any she had ever experienced. She could not stop her lips from opening and feeling his hot tongue drive into his mouth. As his passionate kiss broke she gasped for air.

"Hurry! Fuck me here before they let people into the theatre." Roger almost fell to the ground pulling his pants down. His massive cock was as hard as stone and Lori barely saw it as she turned and bent over with her hands on the bench. She felt his eager hands pull up her skirt and then he grabbed her ass cheeks and leaned into her to mount his wife in this public place.

"Oh God!" Lori cried out as Roger drove his rock hard cock completely into her in one thrust. She could not remember ever feeling him this hard. He was like a wild animal and this was the animal she had missed.

"Baby, I am going to fuck you so hard," Roger moaned, and he was already all over that promise. He thrust into her with an urgency of a wild man. Again and again, that big cock filled his wife's hole. The crowds began to gather at the doors. "Oh my God baby, here it comes!" He moaned, trying not to shout.

His climax was like a volcano erupting with huge surges of white hot cum filling Lori's pussy. He must have pumped 5 or 6 huge streams of cum into her, moaning and leaning into her body to feel her tits from behind. "Hurry Roger, they are about to come in."

Lori was ready. She pulled out a towel and wiped his cock quickly so the wet from her pussy did not stain his pants. She pushed the small towel into her slit to catch the ooze of cum that was already coming out of that stretched pussy. Then she pulled on a pair of panties and they found their seats.

A Holy Thing

Lori felt like such a dirty girl and it was the best feeling she had had in 20 years. The fire was definitely back in her marriage and she had every intention of stoking that fire. She could feel the lust for her bubbling around inside of Roger. But she played it cool and did not just go off the deep end with a non-stop orgy of sex all weekend. They were parents after all.

Sunday morning was always a busy time. Getting Betsy and Jordon off to Sunday school and then the worship service and going to their adult class was a big part of their lives. In the back of her mind, however, Lori could not forget what a wild time she had with her husband at the theatre. She had to remind herself that she is filled with desire for her own husband and that is not sinful. It was hard to shake the idea that she was a bad girl and she was not sure she wanted to.

All through the sermon, Lori wiggled about how hot Roger was. She had the evil urge to get on his lap and let him fuck her right there in church in front of everybody. But fantasy is not reality and she knew better than that.

Sunday school was over early and Roger and Lori went to the van. The kids knew to meet them there rather than try to connect in the busy hallways of the church. Lori had on a pretty white church dress that showed leg up to just above the knee. It had a flowered print that was in step with the season. While she loved her church friends, she was glad to have a few moments alone with Roger.

"Did you like the sermon?" She asked him.

"There was a sermon?" He said with a smile. She knew what he meant. Like Lori, Roger was having trouble thinking of anything else but their wild sex romp on Friday night. Lori turned in her seat and brought her legs under her looking at her handsome husband.

"I think Cathy has the hots for you." She teased him because Cathy was always friendly to everyone and gave kisses on the cheek to her church friends.

"Cathy does not have the hots for me. She is just a friendly girl," Roger said good-naturedly. Just then, Lori reached over and put her hand on his leg just below the crotch.

"She may not have the hots for you but I do." Lori leaned in and whispered in her ear. "I want to do something very dirty to you." She hissed, letting the air stroke his earlobe. Right away Roger's erection sprang to life in his church pants. Slowly Lori moved her fingers over the fabric feeling that hard shaft in his pants and then she found the zipper and pulled it slowly down.

Roger was gasping for air from shock and excitement. "Oh God, Lori, we're at church," he moaned.

"We are not in church." She whispered as she reached in and moved his underwear aside. "We are near it and we are all alone."

"But Sunday school will be out soon. Everybody will be coming out. Our kids..." he objected.

"Then let's not waste any time." She answered. When she pulled out his long, hard dick, Lori was once again amazed how hard it could get. Except for at the theatre, it had been years since she saw or felt him this turned on. Lori and Roger were very conservative people so everything she tried was new to both of them. She had never had her mouth on a hard penis and he had never felt that. But holding that huge manhood as church people milled about the parking lot, there was no time like the present to learn.

"Now you just keep watch," she whispered, kissing his ear and down his neck. She looked down at that erection jutting out of his church pants and slowly got in position to lower her mouth to it. As Roger began to realize what was happening, all he could do was moan in a low tone. "Oh God." That seemed somehow appropriate for Sunday morning.

Lori had planned this, although the idea of doing it to him in the van outside of church was a new twist. She had done some reading and watched a few videos on the internet so she would know what to do. She was trying so hard to be a sex kitten that she kept hidden from her husband that she was nervous about putting his hard cock in her mouth.

Face to face with the monster, Lori felt unsure of what to do. She began with a lick, drawing her tongue from the base of the head to the opening. Her licking turned on her husband, who moaned from that.

"Oh God, there's Felicia," Roger said stroking Lori's hair. "It's ok, she just waved." Roger was just as excited and nervous, and the worry about being caught only excited them both all the more. "Hurry babe," Roger gasped. That moment of waving at Felicia added to the urgency.

Gathering her courage, Lori opened her lips wide and lowered her open mouth onto Roger's hard cock. Her beloved husband moaned almost too loudly feeling her wet mouth close on him and begin to suck. Lori was overwhelmed at the taste of her husband's hard penis and without thinking, he seemed to be pushing it in and out of her mouth. She decided to just go with it and move her mouth instep with him as she learned online.

Lori's head moved up and down in her husbands lap, letting her tongue stroke his hard erection inside her mouth as his hands guided her head. "Oh babe, I'm close." Lori was ready. She had another trusty hand towel ready to go. But she had seen a video about swallowing and she wanted to put plenty of spice into this wild adventure.

Moving her hands up his legs over his church pants, Lori found his testicles and gently began to massage them. As she lowered her mouth onto Rogers hard prick as far as she could stand it and stroke his balls, that was all it took. Roger arched back as if he was going to burst out of his seat and pushed his hips up. Then an enormous orgasm surged out of his hard cock.

Even from watching the videos, Lori was

shocked by the feel of the powerful spurts of cum inside her mouth. Quickly she brought her towel up to her chin so try to keep the overflow from going onto Roger's church pants. His cum was hot and gooey as it spurted onto the back of her tongue. Lori resisted the urge to spit, and instead sucked it toward her throat and swallowed. It was salty and went down in an ooze, coating her throat.

"Oh God, oh God, oh God," Roger moaned. "I am cumming in your mouth," he said with a shocked tone. His hips and testicles convulsed as his orgasm kept coming. Finally, Lori had to take the big penis out of her mouth and cover it with the towel to soak put the rest. From there it was a mad scramble to put him and herself back together before the good church people could get suspicious.

Lori You Are Such a Slut!

"I wondered where you two went at church on Sunday," Cyndi said roaring with delight at the stories of Lori's seduction of Roger. Lori was glad she had the house to herself on Monday to tell her best friend all about it. "Lori you are such a slut!" Cyndi squealed.

Lori laughed out loud at that. She blushed several shades at that term and then smiled, because part of her sort of liked being called a slut.

"In the parking lot of the church!" Cyndi

continued. "Were you out of your mind?" She laughed. "Wait until I tell Steven!" Steven was her husband.

"You better not!" Lori scolded her friend.

"How has Roger been since you started all this? Are things better in bed?" Cyndi wanted to know.

"Unbelievable, girl." Lori answered. "I have not seen him this eager for sex since we first met. It is as if he can't get enough of me. The night after the theatre, we did it twice when we got home!"

"Shut UP!" Cyndi insisted. "If Steven ever tried it twice, I would have to call 911. You are such a slut for coming up with this evil plan!"

"Hey it was your idea, you slut!" Lori teased her friend back. "Maybe you need to accost Steven in public."

"I am inspired. I wonder if I should flash him in court." Cyndi wondered, because Steven was a lawyer. It was sinful to tell Cyndi about her wild sex with Roger but she was bursting with the need for someone to talk to about it. Lori chuckled talking to her BFF, knowing that the whole thing meant Steven was in for the fucking of his life as well.

"Do you have plans for another surprise for that poor husband of yours?" Cyndi asked.

"Not sure but we may have one more big one in us." Lori said.

"If you have one more big one in you, you will get a big one in you." Cyndi said while laughing.

"Bad joke, but that's right!" Lori laughed.

One More in Her

Lori's next seduction of her sexy man caught both of them by surprise. The entire experiment had changed her from the inside out. She was thinking and acting like a horny teenage girl and loving it. She made an extra effort to always look great for Roger because both of them were ready and up for anything. Above all, she always carried that trusty hand towel because the mood might strike at the grocery store, the library, or just about anywhere.

In an effort to make sure they were still sweethearts and not just fuck buddies, Lori agreed with Roger that for her birthday, they would have a picnic at the park. She loved that park because it had a huge open field that was always well mowed and great for kids flying kites, chasing their dogs, or playing Frisbee.

It was nothing but a wholesome setting, but Lori dressed to please her man anyway. She never wanted to get to where she didn't try her best to look sexy for him. That is how things got so bad before and this new era of wild horniness was wonderful for their love affair. It was just a matter of keeping it going.

Lori wore a blue sundress that showed off her legs nicely. It was cut low in front and she did not wear a bra. Her tan had come in well, so to borrow a popular line, she was sexy and she knew it. When Roger swung by the house after work and she came out in that hot outfit, he whistled.

"Am I expected to behave myself with you looking like that?" he said with an evil grin.

"Yes you are you horny dog." She answered, smiling happily at his lust for her. "This is a public park and we are going there to be nice people, not porn stars."

"You are hotter than any porn star babe," Roger complimented. She frowned at his advances, but inside Lori was thrilled.

They found a nice spot where they could be alone, but there were people in sight so they would behave the way normal Christian parents are supposed to behave. They got busy laying out the food and the sheet for the picnic and tried not to lust for each other. That was hard to do. Roger's eyes were constantly going to Lori's legs or trying to get a peek down her top like a horny school kid. Lori was no better giving him ample peeks like, as Cyndi phrased it, "such a slut." But she was a slut for her husband.

While Roger was getting the food out, Lori looked around the park. There were about seven or eight groups scattered far apart from each other. She looked closely and there were no children. It made sense. The park was across from City College so mostly students or young adults were there. Families with kids went to the other parks that had playgrounds and pools. This park was designed for older family fun.

As they enjoyed their food, Roger stared

without shame at his wife's sexy tanned legs. "Babe," he said, "You have never looked so sexy. And you do it without even trying." Little did he know how much work went into looking sexy like she wasn't even trying. But it was worth it. "I sure want to see up that sexy skirt."

How could she say no? She sensuously parted her legs and he got a beautiful look at his wife's sexy pussy. Once again, she "forgot" the panties at home. Lori watched her husband's crotch as that bulge surged into existence like Old Faithful. Suddenly Roger was on the move. He climbed onto his hands and knees and was moving toward the sexy date he had with him in the park.

"Roger, this is not the place. What are you going to do?" Lori said cautiously.

"I just want to kiss my wife." He said with a sexy growl. He got to her and leaned in, and gave her a long wet kiss with his tongue slipping into her mouth deeply. At the same time, his right hand pushed that cute skirt up and the fingers went right into her pussy. Right in the middle of the kiss Lori gasped feeling his skilled fingers part the lips of her cunt and stroke her clit expertly.

Lori's tongue jutted into his mouth as she laid back for him to get on top of her. Roger had no control anymore. He pulled down the top of her dress and Lori's left breast popped out, the cherry colored nipple already hard and ready to be sucked by her man. Roger kissed down her neck biting and sucking.

"Oh God, Roger, it's a family park. There are people!" Lori moaned, but was unable to stop arching up to his love making right there front of everyone. She looked sideways and people were beginning to stare. That only excited her more.

Then she heard his hand working his pants. By the time she was able to look, he had them open and his huge hard-on was dangling down ready to mount his woman. "Roger it's not right. There are people watching!" Lori objected.

"That's what makes it so hot!" Roger almost shouted and he pushed her skirt up revealing her shaved pussy to anyone close enough to see it.

Quickly Lori turned over under the horny man but that didn't slow him down one bit. He pulled her naked butt up to him and mounted her like a stallion stud. "Oh God!" Lori cried out in pleasure when she felt Roger's huge erection spread her vagina rim and plunge inside of her. He began fucking her furiously on the picnic blanket immediately.

He was like a wild animal once again but with even less control. People were shouting and she sensed them beginning to come their way. "Fuck me deep darling, faster faster!" She cried feeling her massive orgasm approaching. Instinctively she arched her butt up to the hard fucking she was taking inside her hole. Suddenly her orgasm hit and she cried out without holding back

"OH OH OH OHHHHHHHHHH," Her cries rang across the park. She heard alarms like the police had been called.

"Hurry, he is raping her!" People were

shouting and running that way. Her orgasm howls of delight were being misunderstood as distress.

"CUM NOW ROGER!" She cried out loudly and he obeyed. He pushed up on his arms and virtually screamed as his balls constricted, forcing a surge of cum to fill his wife's vagina like a tidal wave. He came and came and came inside her just as the onlookers and police showed up.

Roughly, Roger was pulled off of Lori and someone hit him in the face. "Get him. He is a rapist! Take him away." The people cried out as the police pulled him to his feet with his wet hard cock still waving in the breeze.

As he was carried off to jail from the protective cries of the throng people of their town, Roger called out to his lover, "LORI, COME GET ME!"

"I WILL MY DARLING!" Lori called back to her lover to end all lovers. "I WILL!"

2 THE CONCERT OF A LIFETIME

Prologue

There was no bigger band in 1964 than Mute Elephant. They got lumped in with the British invasion, but for millions of fanatic fans, especially college girls, there was no more exciting act to go to see live. A big part of what drove the girls wild about Mute Elephant was their lead singer, Robbie Falco. Falco simply oozed sex with every dance step and every note he sang. He had such a powerful libido that came out in his performance that it was not uncommon for girls to pass out or even orgasm right in their seats.

For Elizabeth and Anna, getting the chance to see Mute Elephant in concert would be the most exciting moment of their year. They were already having a pretty great year getting to go to college at NYU together and be roommates and explore New

York without having their parents hanging around. The girls could trace their friendship back to elementary school, so having their first big adventures away from home together made their freshman year at school perfect. They both turned 18 last April before school so they were ready to take on the world.

Elizabeth was the taller of the two girls, with black hair that she wore to her shoulders. She was noted for her long sexy neck and her slender body. While she hated her small bust line, many boys went wild for her sexy look and she had even been offered with modeling jobs. Anna was shorter and rounder in a sexy way. Her breasts were bigger and her hips shapely, but she was still considered one of the hottest girls to graduate from Central High School in Wilkes-Barre, Pennsylvania, the year before.

Scoring The Tickets

Anna burst into the apartment so excited she could barely contain it. "Elizabeth, I think we can get tickets to the Mute Elephant show!" she squealed with excitement.

"Oh my God! Oh my God! Oh my God!!!" Anna heard her friend explode with excitement, running to her from the bedroom, dancing like a five-year-old. They danced in a circle for a good five minutes, mostly giggling and screeching "Oh my God!"

"Show them to me!" Elizabeth said with a giggle.

"No, I don't have them yet. We have to go to get them," Anna answered.

"Who are you getting them from?" her roommate continued.

"You know the professor in our Intro to Literature class? His name is Dr. Russell? He has some he will sell."

"Oh my God," Elizabeth giggled. "I love him!"

"Me too!" Anna responded. "Get your purse."

Dr. Russell's apartment was in Greenwich Village so it was not far for the girls to walk to. It was on the third floor of a very cool old building that probably was home to poets and artists over many decades. Anna had the address so they found their way to the front door with excitement and rang the bell.

Both girls had dressed cute in outfits that emphasized their sexy features. Elizabeth wore a tube top and a short skirt to show off her long tan legs. Anna wore a light dress that was not as short but emphasized her round butt and allowed her ample cleavage to show. As they walked the streets of New York, they felt the eyes of college boys and professional men turn to admire the view. They liked that feeling of being sexy and on their own in the city.

The door opened and a beautiful middle-aged woman smiled at the two girls. "Hello," she greeted the girls. "I am Mrs. Russell. You must be students of my husband. Alan mentioned that he had some tickets for the concert for you. Please come in."

The girls entered the tasteful apartment and felt good to be welcomed so nicely by Dr. Russell's wife. She showed them to his office, which was a big room full of books and a view to the street in front. There was a nice couch where both girls sat to wait for their professor.

"I must run an errand but Alan will be with you shortly. So nice to meet you both," Dr. Russell's wife said, and as they waited, they heard her leave the building and get in a car that was parked across the street and drive off. After a few minutes, the door opened and their professor came in.

"Anna and Elizabeth. Good to see you. Are you excited about the concert?" he said, smiling and putting them at ease, showing that he was just as nice as he seemed. He sat in a chair opposite of them and his eyes made eye contact with each girl. But instantly his eyes then went to their legs, admiring their sexy look openly.

"Oh yes, Dr. Russell. Thank you so much for letting us come over on a Saturday." Anna said cheerfully. Elizabeth picked up on his mildly flirtatious eye contact and smiled, then flipped her hair. In her mind, she explained to herself, a little sweetness and flirting might help things go better.

The professor reached in his pocket and produced two tickets to the Mute Elephant concert. "Ok girls. That will be $100 each ticket."

Anna and Elizabeth gasped at the price. It was a sold-out show, but that was a lot of money to two college girls in 1964. "Oh I had no idea it would be so much," Anna said with despair. But Elizabeth turned on the charm, turning so Dr. Russell could see her legs even better.

"Please Dr. Martin. We don't have that much money. We're just freshmen at NYU and it's so expensive," she said with her best little girl smile as he gazed at her pretty face. Then she saw his eyes go to her legs again. Elizabeth was running on instinct only, but when those eyes reached her legs, she pulled her feet back, arched her back, and let her legs open. Dr. Russell's face went flushed when he got a gorgeous view up Elizabeth's skirt of her sexy pink panties that conformed nicely to the shape of her pussy. "Can I see the tickets?" Elizabeth said with a coo.

Anna got up and walked to the window. As her professor walked over to sit next to Elizabeth, it was not hard to see the huge bulge in his pants. The 41-year-old professor sat next to his sexy 18-year-old student and put the tickets in her hand, looking at her sexy shoulders. The natural seductive woman in her took over, and she almost whispered to the excited man, "Do you like my legs?"

At this point, Dr. Russell was a goner. He could not even answer as he was so stirred up by the two sexy girls in his den. He put a hand on Elizabeth's leg and slowly began to stroke up her thigh higher and higher. The feeling drove Elizabeth crazy. For the professor, sweat began to ooze out of his forehead. Anna saw that the bulge in his pants seemed to be throbbing.

Elizabeth leaned into her professor's body and looked into his eyes. Almost by instinct more than trying to seduce her, he kissed her mouth and his tongue thrust into her lips instantly. That hand on her leg was under her skirt moving toward her panties fast. The other hand pulled down her tube top and her sweet small breasts were all his. Almost at the same time, he got her skirt up and pulled the crotch cloth aside so he could feel inside her pussy lips, pleasuring her and himself.

Anna watched as the man they both respected so much pushed his finger into her best friend's slit. Elizabeth put her head back and moaned with pleasure as he found her clit and stroked it expertly. Anna was drawn to that couch as if it were a powerful magnet, and when she got there, she plopped down on the other side of the horny professor. She looked around just in time to see his big finger disappear inside of Elizabeth's pussy up to the knuckle. Elizabeth gasped "Oh God, YES" and thrust up to his finger. But she could barely move because of the man's lips on her nipples licking and sucking them eagerly.

The professor had enjoyed fantasies of sexy student girls coming to his home or office for wild sex. But he had never been bold enough to do anything about it. His heart was running out of control and he feared it would burst. But in the back of his mind, he said to himself, "Go ahead. At least you will die happy."

Anna looked down at her friend's pussy being fingered like she was hypnotized. Her fingers worked the zipper of her professor's pants eagerly so she could be part of the fun. She unzipped his pants, reached into his underwear, and found his rock-hard cock pressing against her palm. Skillfully she brought it out so it was jutting out of his trousers.

It wasn't the biggest penis Anna had ever seen, but it excited Anna even more to see it standing up ready to fuck Elizabeth. Anna moved her hand up and down the shaft as precum oozed onto her fingers.

The professor moaned from all of the sensations of tasting Elizabeth's mouth and tits, his finger deep in her cunt and the other sexy coed stroking his cock. He was doing things that he never thought he would do. Suddenly he hardened his own voice and moaned into the ear, "I want to fuck you."

Elizabeth opened her eyes and looked at Anna to find her lowering her face to suck that hard cock. They made eye contact and Elizabeth mouthed, "Oh my god!"

Anna snickered softly and mouthed back. "I know! Do you want to fuck him?"

Elizabeth was on fire with want, but she was nervous about this all going so fast. She was close to orgasm from that fingering, but the small voice of good sense made her mouth say "No" back to her horny friend. Then she glanced down at his sexy cock and to her so Anna knew what to do.

Anna licked the precum from the tip of

the professor's hard cock and then down the shaft. Holding the stiff cock in her fingers, she angled it back and then took the head in her mouth and sucked it softly. Feeling his hard cock in the mouth of the pretty coed pushed the professor even further into heaven than he had been. He sat back and moaned loudly, which let Elizabeth pull her tank top back up.

Elizabeth leaned over, kissed his ear, and sucked his neck as Anna's mouth began to move expertly up and down on his throbbing cock. Anna looked over and Elizabeth had her legs wide open; her own finger was moving up and down the slit of her pussy and massaging her clit to bring herself to orgasm. Anna reached over and ran her hand up her friend's leg, feeling the soft skin of her thigh.

"I'm going to cum!" the professor moaned profanely, holding onto Anna's hair as she sucked him deep in her mouth. Elizabeth took the professor's hand and put it on her tit as Anna slid her mouth over the top of his cock, then licked down to his testicles, and began to lick and suck them.

Elizabeth felt his orgasm hit in how hard he squeezed her left boob, but Anna was not able to get out of the way fast enough. Huge streams of white cum shot out of the end of his cock and landed on her hair and dress. Some ran down his hard cock and she licked it.

The professor shot three times in a row and then opened his eyes to look at Elizabeth. The sweet girl kissed his mouth and he orgasmed twice again. Just then Anna heard a car door slam outside.

"Your wife is home!" she gasped and all three of the excited NYU citizens scrambled.

The girls got the tickets for free.

The Concert

To Anna and Elizabeth, it seemed like an eternity until the day of the concert was to arrive. Their plan was to take the subway to the concert location and then the shuttle thereon. The girls put just as much thought into what to wear and they spent a whole day trying things on to look their best for the show.

It was when Anna walked out of the closet with a very sexy outfit on that Elizabeth knew they had their winner. Both girls wore the shortest skirts possible and skimpy panties. Instead of tube tops, which worked so well to seduce Professor Russell, they wore small T-shirts that ended just below the breasts so they showed maximum skin. Wearing no bra meant they could flash the band easily, which was definitely part of the plan.

Giddy with excitement, the girls locked the door to their apartment to walk to the subway stop. Suddenly Elizabeth squealed with excitement and Anna turned around to see why. In front of their apartment building was a long white limo and a handsome driver leaning against the front hood.

"Good afternoon ladies," the driver said politely. "This is for you." And he handed Anna a card. She ripped it open and read it to Elizabeth.

"Hi girls. Enjoy this limo to and from your concert. Have a great time. You deserve it." It was signed by Professor Russell.

Both girls giggled at the generous gift from their teacher. "I feel like such a whore," Anna said with a delighted laugh.

"Just get in the limo, you whore." Elizabeth teased, slapping Anna on the butt as she crawled in ahead of her.

The concert was in one of the biggest venues in the New York area, but Elizabeth and Anna managed to work their way down close to the front. They were crushed between the other fans of Mute Elephant so it was almost impossible to move. By the time the girls made it to the front of the stage, they were getting used to feeling fingers on their tits and asses.

"Oh my god, Elizabeth!" Anna shouted over the roar of the crowd just before the show started. "The guy behind me has my skirt up and is feeling my ass!" Elizabeth looked past Anna and there was a gorgeous and muscular black guy pressed against her with his hands on her ass, squeezing them and pulling the cheeks apart.

"Anna, he is gorgeous!" Elizabeth yelled in her ear.

"Oh god, his finger is in me!" Anna said, leaning back. Elizabeth pressed against her friend until their tits were meshed together. She looked down to see that huge sexy dark-skinned Adonis unzip his pants and pull out the biggest cock she had ever seen. Anna's eyes were closed and she was moving in rhythm with that big black finger that was inside her.

"Anna," Elizabeth shouted in her ear, "he has his cock out and it's amazing. The concert is about to start. But you are about to get fucked by a huge black cock."

The look on Anna's face was priceless. But the lights were going down. To save the situation, Elizabeth took a drastic move. She was already pressed against her friend so she just grabbed Anna by the hair and pressed a deep wet kiss on her lips. Anna looked like she had seen a ghost as that kiss filled her lips with her friend's lips and tongue.

Elizabeth had trouble stopping that kiss when Anna started sucking her tongue. Finally they stopped and Anna hugged her tight. So Elizabeth gave the gorgeous man with the impressive phallus a look and mouthed to him, "She's all mine." That did the trick.

Robbie Falco Takes The Stage

After a warm-up act, the time came for Mute Elephant to take the stage. The buildup was amazing. Both Elizabeth and Anna wanted to be on someone's shoulders so they would be seen by the band. Anna had no trouble getting two high school kids to hold her up just for the fun of having a girl on their shoulders. When Elizabeth was frantically looking around, she suddenly felt she was being lifted high by very strong hands.

"Don't worry. You are safe," the deep but soft voice said, and it was that beautiful black man that had been fingering Anna. He lifted Elizabeth as if she weighed nothing and put her securely on his shoulders.

Mute Elephant took the stage with an explosion of lights, smoke, fire, and energy. Their music was fast paced and loud and the screams of Anna and Elizabeth were lost in all the noise. The girls had the time of their lives. Robbie Falco was a rock god up there on stage. He strutted around in white pants, red suspenders, and that's all. The pants were very tight and Anna and Elizabeth were close enough to see that the huge bulge in his pants was no stage prop.

Several times during the show Falco leaned over the stage hissing and seducing the crowd. His gorgeous big teeth had a gap in them, and when that long skinny tongue shot out, Elizabeth was certain it was forked. The show was packed with their hits. Finally during one of their big hits, "Feel Me Up," Falco strutted right on the edge of the stage and looked right at Anna. It was her perfect chance so just as he was looking at her, Anna pulled up her top to reveal her glorious breasts. The nipples were hard and pointed right at the sexy rock star.

Falco jumped back. He had seen a lot of tits flashed at him, but he let his long tongue slide out and lick his lips, looking at Anna's. Then he pointed at Anna and glanced to the side to a roadie and strutted away.

"Elizabeth," Anna shouted back at her friend seated on that huge black stallion of a man. "Falco likes my tits. I think they want us!" she screamed with delight. It was a well-known part of the Mute Elephant lore that during the song "Feel Me Up," half of the band left the stage for a break while the drummer and lead guitarist kept the crowd rocking with a long solo set. The lore goes that they go under the stage and invite girls or women they want to fuck. A little orgy is said to happen under there.

That time came in the show. Just as Robbie Falco left the stage, Anna got a signal from that roadie to come with him to be with the sexy rock star. Anna screamed and yelled back to Elizabeth to come with her. Both girls dove off of their perches on their boys to ride the tops of the crowd to the stage. Anna was carried along comfortably facing up, allowing each person who passed her to feel her up.

Elizabeth hit the crowd but there was a mix-up. She twisted and suddenly felt herself falling....

Under The Stage

Anna looked back for Elizabeth but she was nowhere to be seen. She was worried about her friend, but the rush of bodies to that space under the stage swept her away. It was hard to know what was happening, but as soon as the door was closed, she felt her skirt slide down along with her panties and she was nude. The big room was full of pot smoke and there was alcohol everywhere.

A small greasy-looking guy found her and planted a big sloppy kiss on her mouth. Anna did not recognize him but she kissed him back and did not get mad when she felt his finger push into her pussy hole. Suddenly they were forced apart and she looked up at the godlike figure of Robbie Falco himself.

"She's for me," he said in a commanding voice, pushing the smaller guy aside. "Ah my tits girl," Falco said and he picked her up and laid her on a huge pillow-like bed.

"I want you so much," he whispered and his voice was full of song just like when he performed. He was needy and dominant, and Anna wanted to give him anything. He kissed her like he owned her mouth, almost seeming to use it like food as much as for a kiss. He sucked her lips hungrily and pushed down those sexy white performance pants.

"I want to fuck you so hard," the rock star moaned, and Anna just moaned with passion. She barely got a glimpse of that long white cock as it moved toward her pussy but she opened her sexy thighs wide open to take all of him inside. He mounted her with the urgency of a horny beast and pushed that huge rod into the rim of her vagina forcefully.

Anna was fully wet when he entered her, but still she arched up as his massive cock stretched her insides. She knew he had to go fast because the solo was short. He fucked her furiously, sucking her nipples and biting her neck. It was like he wanted to possess her body and her soul. She felt his hands pulling on her butt and she loved feeling that flesh being forcefully taken. Suddenly his finger found its way into her anal hole and push into it.

Anna had not felt that before so the pain caused her to cry out so that others at the orgy looked over. But the pain of that violation mixed with the huge surges of pleasure as Robbie fucked her deep and hard. She orgasmed with such power she was afraid she would buck him out of her. But that pushed him over the edge and he shot a full load of rock star cum inside her.

Elizabeth Understands Security

When Elizabeth woke up, she did not know at first where she was. She remembered the concert, but wherever she was was quieter. She could hear the music not far away, but she knew she was not in the middle of that crowd. She sat up and felt a little dizzy.

"Easy now." She heard a low male voice say as big gentle hands helped her up. As she got used to the light, she saw she was in a smaller room that was like an office with a couch in it. Then she saw a sign over the door that said "Security."

"Am I in trouble?" she asked the voice behind her.

"No, I saw you fall when you were on my shoulders in the concert so I brought you here so you would be safe," he answered. Elizabeth turned around on the couch or bed and looked into the sweet handsome face of that big black hero that held her up above him during the show. On his sleeve, there was an emblem that said "Security."

Elizabeth looked into that gorgeous face and felt her heart stir by how gentle he was in the middle of the debauchery of a rock concert. He was like a dark-skinned handsome prince. His features were gentle, and he had a slight accent like he was from Jamaica.

"You saved me," she whispered softly, placing her soft palm on his face.

The handsome security man placed his big hand over hers. "The important thing is you are OK and safe alone here with me."

"You are like the handsome prince that saved the maiden," Elizabeth said emotionally. "Now your reward will be a kiss."

She leaned forward and gently kissed his lips. Elizabeth had never kissed a black man before, and as he parted his lips for the kiss to become wetter, she felt like they were being swept away with feelings. The kiss did not end as their lips opened and she felt his tongue explore her lips. Elizabeth wound her arms under his and moaned softly, tasting his tongue and sliding hers forward as well.

Gently he lowered her to the soft couch and kissed her deeply; his hands were strong but gentle as he rubbed her back. When that kiss ended, the strong and handsome stranger sucked her neck and slid his hands up her sides, feeling her soft skin. He was so big and strong, and she being so slender, she felt like he was taking her over.

He was gentle but sure of what he wanted. He lifted off her top and lowered his broad face to her small breasts. His pink tongue licked her nipples and then he began to suck. Elizabeth moaned and held his head, feeling emotions and excitement she never had with a boy before.

Moving under him, she pulled up her skirt and pushed down her panties. "Please take me," she moaned to her lover. He was skilled in his movements, sliding her panties off and unzipping his fly. She had seen that big penis but had no idea how much she would want it to fuck her.

He was a large and powerful man, but he held himself so his weight did not crush her as he lay on top of the tiny white girl he wanted so much. That big hard cock was slapping between her bent legs as he got in position to drive it deep into her. He kissed her deep as the head of that huge erection found her slender opening. He pressed and moved so it rotated in her rim, widening it. Then it popped inside and Elizabeth arched back, pushing her nipples to his mouth as she felt herself stretch to take his hard cock.

He filled her up inside, kissing her and whispering how pretty she was and how much he wanted her. His thrusts were powerful but controlled. Elizabeth locked her feet over his broad black back and thrust up to meet the penetrations of his big cock.

"Fuck me," Elizabeth moaned, kissing his ear. "Fuck me deep."

His thrust began to speed up and he held onto her neck, sucking it and pounding his huge cock in and out of her. Suddenly he bit her shoulder a bit and moaned, "I am going to cum in you."

"Oh god yes, fill me up," Elizabeth gasped out of her mind with passion. As his intense fucking speeded up, she arched into him and had a massive orgasm. His climax matched hers and he pushed up and buried that big cock in her and shot load after load of sperm in her.

3 THE CREATURE IN THE FOREST

Prologue

Olivia did her best to settle into passing the summer with her uncle Edmund. Her parents often had to go on tour to the Far East with business, and Edmund's castle was elegant and safe for the young girl. She often spent time there, but she thought that when she turned 18, she would not need his help. Still in all, his big castle was not far from London, so there were many opportunities to shop or have a day of fun in the city.

Every castle seems to have its lore and scary stories, and her uncle Edmund was no different. The stories of a creature in the forest who was part wolf and part man seemed to never die out. Uncle Edmund explained that those stories have been around for centuries, and there had even been sightings, but nothing to give the stories enough credit for the authorities to try to track down the creature.

Olivia had stayed at the castle many summers since she was a little girl, and she had learned many of the secret ways to get around it. Old castles are like that, and she was pretty certain that even Uncle Edmund did not know all of those secrets. It was always fun for her to "disappear" into one of those hidden hallways and reappear elsewhere, almost by magic.

The Servant Girl

The other side of that kind of play is that Olivia often saw things that went on in the castle. Not long after she settled in, she found her way to the dining room where Uncle Edmund was having his afternoon meal. He was not aware that Olivia was looking on. The servant girl brought him his food and attended to him. She was a pretty girl by the name of Suzanne. She had a dark complexion, like she had some relatives from Spain, India, or South America. It added a lot to how pretty she was.

As the pretty servant was clearing some of the food, Olivia's uncle put his hand on hers, and they made eye contact. The servant girl was shy, but the look of desire in her uncle's eye was unmistakable.

"Sir, it's not my station," she said softly as he lifted her hand to his lips to kiss it.

But Uncle Edmund was not convinced that just because she was the servant girl he should observe social rules and leave her alone. He stood up and pulled her to him. "Sir, we could be caught," she whispered, but she was swept away by his want of her.

The weathered land owner stood and pulled the servant girl to his body. The kiss that he put on her lips was possessive and passionate. Olivia gasped and retreated from her hiding place rather than get caught watching the lovers. She did not see what happened next.

Suzanne let herself be molded to the body of her master as he kissed her deeply. She felt his tongue slide into her mouth, and shyly, she let hers explore his lips. Suddenly, the guilt got to her and she tried to pull away.

"But Sir, my husband…" she gasped. The young servant girl was married to James, the chauffeur of the estate. When that passionate kiss aroused her inside, the thought of him brought up guilt and worry. The master of the house was not deterred by her protests. He pulled her to him and kissed her hard, noticing her excitement.

"He belongs to me and you belong to me," the Lord of the estate declared, and he kissed her passionately while pulling her long skirt up. Suzanne's heart was racing as she turned from the kiss and helped her Lord pull up her skirt to reveal her thin white legs.

"Yes my master," she said and the hiss of passion filled the voice of the young servant girl. Edmund turned the beautiful young girl around so she could lean forward on the table with her hands mixed in with the dishes from his meal. He was so forceful that Suzanne felt very much owned by him, and that excited her. When James made love to her, he was tender and gentle. Being taken roughly was such a new world for her.

She braced herself as she felt her master fold her gown over her lips and pull down her panties. Her naked butt and sex was exposed to him for the first time. The lusty Lord leaned in and kissed his servant girl on the neck biting her earlobe. "I am going to fuck you Suzanne." He moaned, pushing his fingers into her butt cheeks and down to the mound of her pussy. Her hole was oozing wetness as it prepared to take the cock of the man who was her master.

Suzanne heard Edmund open his pants to let his hard cock out. She glanced back and saw the obscene vision of that large stiff penis pointing straight out from his body. It was so much larger than that of her sweet husband James. Edmund's passions were driving him wild as he forced her slender legs apart. His rough fingers felt up and down her wet slit and found her clitoris and pinched it.

Suzanne gasped and fell forward on the table as her body responded to his forceful feeling of her cunt. This only caused her to arch her butt up to him to make it easier for him to fuck her. Her master could not be held back any longer. He fell on her and plunged his rock hard cock deep into the little servant girl. He held her around the waist and mounted her like a wild dog. His fucking thrusts filled her tiny hole, stretching it.

Suddenly, Suzanne felt her orgasm hit, and she cried out in moans and weeping sounds. The sound of her orgasm pushed her master over the edge. He rose up, and with a loud cry, he shot his load inside the little servant, filling her vagina with his cum. He shot over and over again until the warm white cream ran down her legs.

As Suzanne gathered her clothing so she could leave the room, she glanced at the window to the dining hall. Just then she saw a stranger looking in. He was a striking beautiful dark-skinned man with jet black hair and dressed like a prince. Just as fast as she saw him, he was gone.

More Than a Vision

Suzanne never said anything to anyone about what happened with her Lord that day. When she discovered that Olivia had moved in, Suzanne was happy for another young woman on the property that was close to her own age. Most of the servants were older men and women so at 21, Suzanne often wished for more people around like herself. But it was not acceptable to be friends with someone outside the servant class.

Mr. Bates was in charge of all of the

servants in the castle. When Mr. Bates met the young Olivia, he saw that it just made sense to assign Suzanne to attend to the young guest of the Lord. During the course of attending to Olivia's needs, Suzanne did share with her what she saw out of that window that day. For some reason when Olivia heard these stories, it excited something in her. It was like somehow she had a spiritual connection to that mysterious stranger that nobody knew was real.

The reports of the strange and very handsome prince being seen looking in windows or strolling on the grounds were common. Olivia had her share of sightings that she kept to herself. In her mind, it was like he was following her. Often, she would suddenly turn to catch a glimpse of that tall and strikingly beautiful figure moving in a doorway or turning down a hallway.

Her dreams were haunted by dark images that somehow mixed the myth of the creature in the woods with that handsome prince that always seems just out of reach. She awoke in a sweat, dreaming of seeing the menacing face of the beast in the dark, his piercing blue eyes staring at her and a low growl of warning coming from his throat.

The most unsettling part of that dream is that she did not feel a sense of doom from the presence of the beast so nearby. She felt an insatiable desire coming from it. She often woke from such dreams and laid there thinking of that low growl and those eyes making her naked in front of him, and her fingers drifted under her gown to slide inside her panties. Her fingers aroused her clitoris thinking of that surge of want coming from the beast. She was far more aroused by it than terrified.

Olivia woke from such a dream unable to lie still. Her heart and loins were on fire. The darkness of the night was broken by a bright moon, which shone through the window of the balcony of her bedroom. That balcony looked down on the courtyard of the elegant castle. Olivia felt she needed the cool night air to chase the phantoms away. She walked to the doors of the balcony and opened them. But when she stepped out, she gasped at the sight.

She often looked at that tranquil courtyard for peace. As she did so, she saw the faces. Dozens, perhaps hundreds, of faces in the dark all around the courtyard. They were not human faces but those of wolves. As she watched, the yard filled with the always moving bodies of full-grown and dangerous wolves. As they circulated, suddenly, the largest beast she could imagine emerged and milled among them. This had to be the fabled beast.

The sight of the beast and his army of wolves just outside her window overwhelmed the young girl. She fell back into her room, pushed the doors to the balcony shut, and locked them. Then she became hysterical, ran to her bed, and buried herself under the covers and wept. She waited to hear the angry mob of wolves to begin to assault the castle seeking to destroy and devour everyone within. But the castle fell silent. Olivia dozed but kept waking to listen for the attack. None came.

What she heard instead was the sound of heavy breathing in the room with her. "The beast is here," her mind said to itself in fear. But her heart was not afraid. Then she heard that heavy breathing create a word that came across the room as a dark whisper of her name—"Olivia." Fearfully, Olivia lowered the blanket and that is when she saw it. But it was not the beast. It was the beautiful prince gazing down at her from the foot of her bed. He was stunningly beautiful with full black curly hair and piercing eyes looking at her. He was shrouded in a long cape that wound around his tall and slender frame.

He walked to the side of her bed just inches from her face. Once again, that whisper came. "Olivia," it said. "You belong to me. You always have." With a jolt, the powerful prince yanked down her blankets, and she lay helpless on the bed with nothing but her slim nightgown to protect her. Just as swiftly, he dropped his cape. His perfect body stood naked before her. His chest was chiselled muscle and the curves of his thighs were like art.

Just in front of her face was his long penis, with perfectly shaped testicles just behind them. It dangled close to her invitingly, and she felt drawn to it as if it was a magnet to her lips. The prince knelt on the bed and that whisper said firmly, but lovingly, "Come to my sex. Make love to it."

Nervously, Olivia fondled the Prince's shaft and stroked the head. It was like making love back; it grew stiff and angled up to her lips. She kissed the hole and let her tongue caress the opening. Olivia was not skilled in love, so this all seemed to come from unspoken commands from this magical prince. It seemed so natural to slide the tip of his royal cock in her mouth and suck it reverently. Just as maidens bow before a king, now Olivia lowered her head and sucked the hard-on of her prince.

The mysterious dark skinned prince mounted the bed with his knees on each side of Olivia's head as he looked down on his long hard cock partly inside her sweet lips. Olivia knew only that she felt complete with his hard member in her mouth, and tried to let more of it go inside until every part of her tongue was tasting it. As she moved her tongue on it and he moved it back and forth, the smooth skin seemed to become rougher, and there seemed to be more hair around the testicles each time her tongue explored there.

"You arc my princess," came the whisper as light as the wind with no human tone it. The intensity of his want for her was overpowering as he leaned into her thrusting into her mouth faster and faster. As Olivia looked up at the man of mystery, he seemed to be getting larger, and suddenly, a growl filled his chest and his eyes looked wild and hungry.

Suddenly, he lunched forward covering her head with his muscular torso and held her jaw as his hard cock seemed to spread out inside her mouth. With a huge grunt, he pulled it out of her lips as gushing sprays of white cum shot from it covering her hair and face. Olivia was confused and frightened, and reached up whimpering, "Hold me my Prince," but the changes were coming so fast.

Before she could understand any of it, his body lunged to the side. The massive beast took the bed from underneath and turned it over away from him, throwing Olivia to the floor. All that Olivia knew of her lover was the sound of a growling howl as he disappeared out the window.

Suzanne and Olivia

Olivia kept in her heart what happened that night, but she had so many feelings as she righted her bed and cleaned the thick cum from her face and hair. Suzanne collected her gown the next day for cleaning, and it was she that noticed the cum stains. But Suzanne had her own secrets to hold so she did not embarrass her mistress.

Olivia was glad to have Suzanne attend to her as she pondered her bonding with the mysterious prince. She and Suzanne had discussed the prince often. The young servant girl did not even mention the prince for some days after wondering about the stains and because she could tell her mistress was distracted.

"They say the beast is angrier now mistress." Savannah said as she combed Olivia's long soft hair after her bath.

"Yes, I hear the howls at night." Olivia answered, remembering what she saw in the courtyard.

"They say the beast seeks his bride," she continued, not knowing the intensity of the events of that night so recently.

"Have you seen the mysterious prince again Suzanne?"

The girls talked about the prince and his strong magnetic draw on both of them without revealing any secrets. Olivia enjoyed the feeling as Suzanne applied soft lotions to her back and arms to make her skin soft and feminine. "Your skin is so pure and unblemished, like a princess," Suzanne said, kneeling at her feet and applying the lotion to Olivia's legs.

After her bath, Olivia was pampered like this by her maidservant, sitting on the bed with only the towel across her lap.

"You flatter me Suzanne," Olivia said in a dreamy state of pleasure as she laid back and let her servant's hands relax her. The attention was soothing after the troubling affairs of late. Olivia felt her legs open so her servant could caress and lotion her thighs.

"You are perfect in every way," Suzanne whispered, captivated by the feel of her mistress's skin against her tiny fingers. Feelings slowly made themselves known that Suzanne had never known before, and she came up on her knees, leaned down, and kissed Olivia's thigh gently. Both girls seemed to be in a trance, which caused Olivia to softly moan and touch her pretty servant girl's soft hair.

Suzanne spread her fingers up those warm soft thighs letting her fingers push the towel away revealing Olivia's delicate folds of her pussy. The hair was light colored and not thick, and the lips were pouty and beginning to stand out because of the attention she was getting.

Suzanne gazed at the untouched pussy of her mistress and felt strange stirrings. She continued to kiss Olivia's legs and then touched the lips of her sensitive area, parting them to view the pink slit. Using the same care and patience she used when she explored her own pussy, Suzanne slid her finger along that pink flesh, noticing the wetness beginning to develop in Olivia's vagina.

Olivia's moans intensified as Suzanne explored how to pleasure her mistress. Finding Olivia's clitoris, she surfaced it and stroked it tenderly. Her kisses were so close to that sweet pussy that she could take in the soft odours of Olivia's wet bottom. Suzanne's curiosity was full as she slid her finger around the opening of Olivia's pussy hole and took some of the wet and then tasted it.

That taste was intoxicating so she leaned in and kissed the open slit and then pleasured the clitoris with kisses and the massage of her tongue. Olivia was moaning and her stomach was rolling with the intensity of her pleasure. "Oh Suzanne, yes," she whispered as the servant girl touched the opening and slowly inserted her finger inside Olivia's vagina.

"Oh my mistress," Suzanne gasped as she felt Olivia's vagina muscles tighten around her finger. Suzanne was filled with new feelings as she leaned forward and lowered her lips to the open mouth of her mistress. Olivia's eyes were closed, and her hips bucked as her servant girl's kiss pressed onto her mouth and their tongues engaged. Just then, the orgasm hit Olivia's pussy, and she bucked up to Suzanne, cumming in powerful spasms around that tiny finger inside her.

Raw Desire

Olivia woke up deep in the night with her servant Suzanne in bed with her. The girls were not able to part after making love. It was not suspicious for a maiden to stay with her mistress in cases of fear or illness. When Suzanne revealed her naked form to Olivia, their lovemaking went on for what seemed to be hours. Finally, after many orgasms, they fell asleep nude in each other's arms.

Olivia slipped out of bed, troubled. She kissed the lovely servant girl on the forehead and pulled on her nightgown to explore. She sensed the closeness of the dark prince without any evidence. She slipped to her balcony, unlatched the doors and stepped out into the cool night air. The courtyard was peaceful with no life moving other than the flowers swaying in the soft breeze. Off in the distance, the forest was full of the howls of the wolves calling out. Their Lord, the beast, must be on the move, Olivia thought.

Olivia waited and then she heard it. As if the wind had a voice, it came as before - the sound of her name. "Olivia" it called out, and she knew it was him. Her stomach churned, unsure how to go to him. Just then, she saw the forest open and he emerged. Dressed in his princely garb, he stepped into the courtyard and gazed up. He did not speak, but from that distance, his piercing gaze made her his own. He turned toward the woods to the path he had come from and looked back at her. She had to follow.

Her feet seemed to fly down the stone steps of the castle, out the door to the courtyard and into the forest, following where she saw his slender form go. The slight trail was no guide, so she let her emotions take her. At each turn, she saw a flair of color - his shirt or his jet-black hair - and she ran for all she could, not trying to remember her way back.

She burst into a field that was exploding with long grass and flowers. Olivia stood gasping for air. Suddenly, the woods were silent from all around. Then he stepped from the brush, gazing at her. His gaze was so intense that it took moments to see that he was nude. She waited for him to approach, but there was no approach.

In a blink, his body was on hers. He was

demanding and forceful, taking her to the forest floor. He knelt over her, and his eyes were at once loving and hungry. There was a wildness about him that was from a place that could not be satisfied. He sat up over her hips, and that long hard penis stuck out again, eager to take his bride.

The prince grasped the sides of Olivia's gown and ripped it in one pull. The fabric shredded like tissue, and her slender nude body was exposed to him and to the woods. Suddenly, a deep inner voice said, "Flee," and Olivia slipped out from under him and dashed into the field. He was on her as fast as the wind bringing her down on to her face in the flowers.

"I must have you," the wind said, saying his will.

"Yes my prince," she cried out. "Violate me!"

Olivia felt his breath as the needy prince bent and pulled her naked body to his own. His mouth was on her neck, and then he forced her head sideways and kissed Olivia's mouth deeply. Olivia felt his long tongue find deep places in her mouth and taste her fluids. She slipped her own tongue to his lips, and he drew it in and sucked it inside his hungry mouth as though it was food.

His mouth was moving, sucking, and biting so often that the pain of his bites turned into passion. He did not open her skin, as his teeth were skilled in how to taste his prey. This time, he felt his breath on her back as he bit and kissed it and commanded her.

"Push your butt up to take my cock, my bride," he moaned with a low growl in his voice. Olivia obeyed and brought her knees up so her tiny butt was offered up for him to molest. She felt his powerful hands grasp her upper thighs and force them open so her pussy was spread for him to make his own. Those hands then grasped her butt cheeks and squeezed them, opening them as well and his finger slid down the crack and caressed her anal opening. Nothing of hers was to be forbidden to him.

Olivia felt the fingers of her prince probe the tender opening of her vagina. His long hard cock was moving back and forth, slapping her thighs and butt as he prepared to violate her. Just then, Olivia looked up, and all around the edges of the clearing she saw wolves gathering. They gazed at the slender girl on the floor of the forest with the powerful prince preparing to fuck her from behind.

Olivia's body was on fire. Her fears were overpowered by want to be his and to feel that powerful cock fill her insides for the first time. As the magical creature of the forest mounted her, he looked up at the wolves and from his deepest places, he growled. As he made those primitive noises, the wolves all began to bark and howl as if to say, "Yes lord, fuck your Queen."

The plunge of his hard cock into her pussy was swift, and the surge of pain caused Olivia to arch her head up and cry out. Her moans of pain and pleasure mixed in with the howls of the wild animals. The wild man mounting her thrust his hard cock into her again and again, fucking her ferociously. The power of his hips was so forceful that Olivia felt he would split her open from the womb out. But that hard phallus kept filling her wet hole, pulling out, and then deep in her so far that it pounded against her cervix deep inside her body.

Suddenly, that cock in her began to spread out and change shape. At the same time, the handsome prince on her growled deeply and grew bigger and more muscular. Olivia looked back at a beastly animal that was fucking her. She then knew for certain that the prince she so adored was the same beast of legend and that now she belonged to him. She would not resist that when he climaxed inside her, she would be devoured.

His voice was no longer human. He growled and made unhuman sounds as his animal like hips pushed that massive beastly cock in and out of her. With a howl that put chills into every man, woman and child for miles, the prince buried his member in his bride and filled her with his seed. Like a river of cum, his balls forced his royal sperm deep into Olivia's violated pussy.

Olivia swooned as she orgasmed around his massive cock and fell forward. As she lost consciousness, she looked back at the sweet and beautiful face of her prince. He was fully human when he was satisfied. When she woke up, she was on the floor of the field naked and fucked. Her pussy was oozing his cum, and she felt tender hands caressing her face.

"Suzanne?" Olivia gasped looking up at her servant girl who loved her mistress after her bridal moment.

"Yes Mistress it is me. I am not just your servant, I am his. You are his queen now, and I will take you to your royal throne. Even now, the prince goes to the castle to destroy the one who holds his property wrongly, the usurper Edmund. But you will bear the seed of the beast within you and give him an heir."

As Olivia felt a movement in her deepest womanhood, she knew the new life in her was the son of the beast. She walked with Suzanne who kissed her mouth and took her to her destiny as new queen of all she surveyed.

4 THE SUPERBOWL PARTY

Preface

Leslie sat on the second row in the classroom and admired her husband as he spoke to the singles group. Leslie and Robert were both 30, but they looked much younger. That is why working with young adults aged 18–24 was a good job for him. And Leslie did all she could to make it work by being the hostess when kids came to their home, and by making friends with the girls so they could open up to her if they needed to.

The talk was about responsibility, and it was impossible for Leslie not to notice the young girls staring at her husband with more than just admiration. At one point, a cute blond by the name of Amber uncrossed her sexy legs so it drew his eyes to her short skirt. When his eye went there, she opened her legs and let him look up her skirt.

Leslie was aware enough of Robert's mind

that she knew he became aroused by Amber. She could even tell he got a hard-on from the bulge in his pants. Robert did not have a large cock, but it was enough to push out his pants. Robert was a driven youth leader, and he knew to not be distracted by that sexy peek at Amber's panties. It is normal for young people to get crushes on their leaders, and Robert was a very good-looking man.

Instead, Leslie knew how to turn it to her advantage. Leslie had a clean-cut look, but she was quite sexy and got plenty of looks from the boys in the youth gatherings as well. She was a slender blond with medium breasts that were perky so they pushed out her dresses nicely. She had slim legs that were tan and sexy so she was able to hold her own with the sexy young girls in the group if she wanted to. But being older, she had the wisdom of how to keep from freaking out when a cute gal gave her husband a peek and even turn it to her advantage.

Leslie's Game

Leslie got home ahead of Robert by a couple of hours. First, she put together a delicious meal that would seduce his nose the minute he walked in for dinner. But her seduction of her husband was far from over. Leslie took the time to pay attention to the skirt little Miss Amber had on when she gave her husband that show. Leslie had an outfit that was just right with a sexy skirt the same length and color.

She took time to shave her legs and pussy so she looked the part of a 20-year-old girl in every way. She even brought home a nametag from the event that day and filled it out so it read, "Hi, I am Amber." This way, there would be no mistake as to what Robert's crafty wife was up to.

When Robert came home, Leslie was in costume but in the kitchen. "Hi honey, go ahead and change clothes for dinner!" She felt so sneaky and that began to get her turned on. She heard the shower running so she brought a couple of folding chairs into the living room and set up a practice podium he used when he was preparing a speech or sermon. When the shower stopped, she slipped into the chair, which faced the podium roughly the way Amber did.

When Robert came out, she stopped him in his tracks at the little scene she had set up.

"Hi big boy," she coocd at him. "Do you want to give your speech about responsibility to Amber privately?" Leslie squirmed in her seat, mocking the sexy little girl who was doing the same for her husband just hours before.

"Leslie, now, I did not come on to..." he stammered.

"Oh Mr. Roscoe, your wife Leslie felt you needed to give that speech to Amber one on one, so she can truly show her admiration for you," Leslie said in a low voice that was playful and sexy.

When it dawned on Robert what his wife was up to, that bulge appeared in his pants. "Ok Amber, the talk is about responsibility," Robert said in his professional voice, but his eyes were firmly on those sexy legs and that very short skirt. He had not spoken very long when Leslie interrupted him by raising her hand and tipping her head to the side and smiling.

"Yes, Amber?" Robert said, acting irritated.

"Mr. Roscoe, I feel I have learned so much from you that I have a responsibility to show you my appreciation," Leslie said seductively. As she said that, Leslie uncrossed her legs and spread them open to give her husband a nice view up her skirt at her thong that was molded into her pussy.

"Now Amber, that is hardly appropriate," Robert said to his wife without blinking as he stared at her almost naked pussy.

"Yes Mr. Roscoe, but you want to fuck Amber don't you?" Leslie said with a coo, and with that, she pulled her skirt up to her hips. "Why don't you take Amber's panties off?"

Robert lost control. He fell to his knees in front of his sexy wife and pushed her legs apart to get to her sexy pussy. "Oh Mr. Roscoe," Leslie said as she felt her body rush with excitement at how turned on her husband was. Robert pulled that thong down and threw it over his shoulder - so far they almost never found it the next day.

Robert pulled Leslie's sexy legs forward in the chair and lowered his face to her open cunt. "Oh god Amber, you have such a sexy pussy," he moaned, and it was then that Leslie knew that in his mind, he really was going to eat out that 20-year-old girl from earlier. She felt strange because this disturbed her, but when his mouth began to eagerly lap her slit and suck her clit, she forgot all about it and became Amber.

"Mr. Roscoe, fuck me right here in the classroom," she gasped as she felt his tongue slide into her wet vagina. As the horny youth leader licked his wife, he eagerly dug at his pants to pull his hard cock out to mount Amber right here in his living room.

"I will Amber. I am going to fuck you," he said in broken gasps pushing his pants down so his hard six-inch cock would be free to penetrate her. Robert fell on his wife and started kissing and sucking her neck and shoulder, squeezing her tits through that blouse she had put on for her costume.

"Do it Mr. Roscoe. Fuck Amber," Leslie gasped when his hard cock slid into her as it had so many times. But he rammed it into her with a force she had never known. For all the confusion of how this was going, Robert had never fucked her this hard before.

His grunts were in sync with each hard push that buried his cock inside Leslie's wet pussy to the balls. Robert grasped her butt and squeezed the cheeks so hard it hurt Leslie as she angled her pussy up to him and hooked her feet over his back. "Oh god Amber!" he cried out and then he pushed up on his wife and filled her with cum. It was only as he was shooting his hot spurts of sperm into this sexy girl under him that Robert began to sort out exactly who he had just fucked.

The Girls Get Ready

The organization that Robert ran was not a church young adult group. Instead, it was a service offered by the community and backed by all of the churches as well as by civic-minded organizations who wanted to help young people meet in a healthy environment where they could also ask questions about their faith. Robert was the perfect leader for this because he was likeable and he had good public-speaking skills. He ran the organization well and he had enough training in religious ideas that he could lead a discussion when that time was appropriate.

It was always fun for Robert and Leslie to plan the big Superbowl party. It was so successful that they split into two locations. Robert would handle the larger group who would use the gym at the Catholic Church, while Leslie hosted a smaller gathering at a home of one of the active families. The day before the party, Leslie stopped and got decorations and food and went on to the home where she would be hosting the party.

This was a great time for the girls of the group to have a hen party. The only thing that made Leslie nervous was the home, because it was owned by the parents of Amber.

Robert and Leslie got past the strange role-playing they did. It wasn't that it wasn't exciting. To Robert it was the best fuck he had ever had, especially with his own wife. Leslie also orgasmed like a wild animal, but her emotions were all over the map. To her, in a way, Robert had fucked Amber. But she could not be mad at him because she had made it happen. It's best to just forget it.

Leslie wore a comfortable sundress with a blue print that showed her legs just above the knee. She had learned to attend these affairs looking cute, feminine, and not like a frumpy minister's wife. As cute as Leslie was, that just took shopping for outfits that were attractive without revealing too much.

She arrived at the home and was relieved that there were a couple of girls there besides Amber. Amber answered the door with a cheerful, "Hi Mrs. Roscoe." Leslie had to remember that the fantasy she played out was not the real Amber. But it was hard not to feel a flood of emotions being in the home of the girl who had started it all with that flirty flash up her skirt. It didn't help things that Amber was wearing that same very short skirt that made her look so very sexy.

Amber and her two friends Whitney and Chloe were full of life and chatter. Amber was a very outgoing girl and made it clear from the beginning that she admired and liked Leslie for her leadership in the group. Before long, Leslie was laughing and feeling like just one of the girls. After about an hour and a half, Whitney got a call that she had to run an errand for her mom. Chloe was her ride.

That left Leslie and Amber alone and that is when Leslie got those feelings again. The thing that was most disturbing to Leslie is how she could not stop looking at Amber's legs that were so cute and sexy in that short skirt. It was the knowledge that her husband looked up that skirt that made those legs so alluring to Leslie. Along with the fact that the sight of her panties up that skirt resulted in such an explosive fucking that Leslie enjoyed as Robert thought he was fucking this little girl. All of that confused Leslie and in a way excited her.

"Mrs. Roscoe, you are so beautiful. I am so glad we are becoming friends." Amber purred as they finished up the last of the decorations. "How about a glass of wine to celebrate?" Amber said.

"Call me Leslie, Amber," Leslie answered feeling herself relax. "A glass of wine would be lovely."

When Amber came back in, she sat opposite of Leslie and they chatted like old friends enjoying their drinks. "I love your outfit Amber," Leslie finally said.

"I noticed you could not keep your eyes off of it," Amber said with a giggle. "Thank you. Yours is very cute too."

"Well, I noticed my husband liked it a lot when he was teaching the other day," Leslie said without any accusation in her voice.

"Oh my god!" Amber suddenly exclaimed, putting her wine down and covering her mouth to giggle loudly. "Did you see that?" She asked. "Leslie, we were just being silly!"

The blush on Amber's face was adorable and it made Leslie giggle too. The wine was kicking in and that made both girls silly. "Yes I did!" Leslie laughed and by that, Amber knew that the pretty wife of her youth leader was not angry. "I think he liked what he saw very much."

Amber was blushing like it was her job. "We were just playing around," she said, breathing hard from the laughing. "But I had panties on Leslie. I swear."

Suddenly, a flush went over Leslie and she seemed to be another person. "I think it is only fair Amber," Leslie found herself saying, "that I see what he saw."

The girls had a moment of intensity as they looked into each other's eyes. Amber smiled softly at what she was about to do. "Ok," she said shyly. "I want you to see." Leslie was tingling all over and unable to look away as Amber leaned back a bit and then began to open her legs. Slowly, the sexy skin of her upper thighs was revealed to the young wife. Finally, she opened them wide enough that Leslie saw Amber's panties.

Leslie stared at the folds of Ambers slight panties that molded around the mounds of her pussy revealing the lips and a slight wetness right over the girl's vagina. Leslie felt her own wetness begin to ooze as she stared at the young girls barely hidden cunt.

"I am so turned on," Amber said in a whisper. "Are you?" She gasped.

"Yes," Leslie said without thinking and she felt dizzy and out of control.

"Open your legs," Amber said staring at Leslie's skirt. Leslie's body obeyed without the good sense in her mind having a chance to vote. As if she was being guided from someone else's mind, Leslie pulled her skirt up to about mid-thigh. Then, shyly she opened her legs and let Amber look up her skirt.

Leslie had on cotton panties but they were so wet from her arousal that they hugged her pussy tightly showing all of her sex easily.

"You are so sexy Leslie," Amber said. "Do you think I am sexy?" she asked, pulling up her skirt so all of her legs were showing.

"Oh god, yes," she answered, following Amber's lead and pulling up her skirt to her hips, so her panties were easily visible. Amber's voice was soft, almost a whisper, and it hypnotized Leslie.

"You have such sexy legs," Leslie heard Amber coo. Leslie was operating on feelings and as that voice seduced her, she slid her hand inside her panties and stroked her clit. Suddenly, she felt hands on her thighs. Opening her eyes, Leslie saw Amber kneeling at her feet. Amber began to feel up Leslie's legs from the knees, moving up and pushing her thighs apart to look toward her barely concealed pussy.

"Mr. Roscoe is so hot," Amber said looking at Leslie's legs and letting her fingers spread up to her panties. "All the girls in the group want to fuck him," she said, moving her fingers over the crotch of Leslie's panties and stroking her pussy lips through the thin fabric. "He fucks this pussy," Amber said in a low voice beginning to pull Leslie's panties down. "I want to watch his sexy cock go inside your hot pussy Leslie," Amber said.

The dirty talk was driving Leslie wild. "Oh god Amber," was all she could moan as the little girl seduced her. The young girl's lips touched Leslie's upper thigh as the panties came off. Leslie looked down at her naked legs wide open and Amber kissing her way up to her pussy. "We have to stop," Leslie said weakly, but when she put her fingers in Amber's hair, she did not push her away.

Instead, Leslie slid down in the big lounge chair and watched as the beautiful girl's lips and tongue reached her pussy. Amber explored Leslie's sexy folds, pulling open her pussy lips so she could see and lick the pink flesh of her slit. But when Amber found Leslie's clit and began to lick it, Leslie moaned loudly and clutched Amber's hair.

That soft tongue massaged Leslie's clit as Amber's fingers stroked her round pussy lips and found Leslie's pussy hole. Just then, Amber looked up at Leslie with her fingers stroking her vagina rim. "He fucks you in here," she said obscenely. "Your husband sticks his sexy cock up in here and fucks you deep," Amber said, gazing up at the face of the woman in ecstasy.

"Oh god yes Amber. He fucks me." Then, Amber pushed her finger deep inside the cunt of her youth leader's wife, licking and sucking her clit. Leslie's stomach muscles were convulsing out of control and her hips thrust up to meet Amber's mouth. Amber licked down to Leslie's vagina and then down further, sucking her pussy lips and even licking her anal hole.

It was when that soft tongue lapped her butt opening that Leslie lost it. Her orgasm exploded and she moaned loudly, cumming hard onto Amber's eager tongue.

The Superbowl Party

Leslie wanted to put all of the wild things that had been going on with Amber and Robert behind her and focus on being a great hostess for the party. The kids started showing up at the house several hours before the game. For quite some time, Leslie did not see Amber but she was nervous about it.

They had not spoken since that intimate experience. After Amber made Leslie cum, they went and laid down on the couch together and kissed. Amber began to feel nervous about what she had done. Leslie comforted her, even though she was so confused about letting a girl do that to her. As they kissed to comfort each other, Amber took Leslie's fingers and guided them to her panties.

Leslie slid her fingers into Amber's panties and found her clit. "Yes Leslie,"

Amber moaned, holding on to her neck. Shaking like a leaf, Leslie stroked Amber's clit and slid her fingers up and down that wet pussy slit. When Leslie found Amber's vagina opening and slid a finger inside her, the young girl began to cum. They held each other tight as Amber orgasmed again and again.

Both girls were confused and nervous about what had happened. Leslie wanted to try to smooth it over so it did not ruin her marriage, or even Amber's participation in the young adults group. They spoke about it by phone, and in the end, they became good friends. The agreement was to keep what happened between them and to not repeat it.

As Leslie prepared the food for the Superbowl party, Amber was her best helper. At times, they would catch each other's eye and smile knowingly or exchange a squeeze of the hand, but that was all friendly. It was the best Leslie could do with a confusing encounter, because keeping the group events working smoothly was important to her and to her husband.

When people started to show up, the Superbowl party pretty much began to run itself. Leslie kicked into the hostess mode, charming both genders equally and it was all quite wholesome. They even took time before the game activities began to have a prayer to give thanks for the food and the fun of being together.

While everyone understood that it was to be in moderation, some beer and wine was included in the fun. The table that was set up for food was soon packed with different snacks and casseroles that each person brought. All of the drama of what went on with Amber and Robert vanished for a while, and Leslie was the good woman again.

Just before kickoff, several of the guys who were regulars to the group arrived. Leslie greeted them, along with a guest they brought by the name of Max. She was impressed with Max because he was stunningly handsome and very polite. He fit right in.

Leslie started to really enjoy herself. Her dad was a big football fan so she knew how to root for the team and enjoy the way the game was played. She had a couple glasses of white wine and snacks from that table of treats without really thinking about what she was eating. She had trouble deciding when to take a break because the commercials were so fun, but finally she had to stand up and stretch her legs. It was then that the rich food and wine caught up with Leslie. As she was crossing the room, a dizzy spell hit her pretty bad and she felt herself begin to pass out.

Leslie stumbled and began to fall. Near her were two girls in the group, Amber and Christina, and they saw the problem. Quickly, both of them grabbed Leslie before she fell into the table of food. Before either Christina or Amber could call out, suddenly Max was there supporting Leslie and keeping her on her feet. Leslie felt the strong hands holding her up and leaned back into his chest.

"I just need to lie down," she whispered. Amber looked at Max and his face was full of concern.

"There is a bedroom at the end of the hall. She can lay down there and it will be quiet," she instructed him. Max began to walk Leslie back when she swooned again. Without thinking, Max picked her up to carry her to where she could recover. Both Christina and Amber gasped at how strong he was and that act of chivalry he was putting on display.

Max carried Leslie into the bedroom and laid her on the bed. He closed the door to cut down on the noise. When he returned, he helped her sit up.

"Any better?" he asked softly.

"My head is swimming," Leslie responded.

"We have to get your blood flowing," Max said out of his knowledge of CPR. "Let's get you out of that dress." He unzipped the pretty green dress in back, revealing her pale smooth back. Max helped Leslie lean forward as he pulled her skirt up and around her small round butt cheeks.

Leslie felt her dress coming off and tried to object through the fog. "Wait..." she said weakly. "Maybe this isn't..."

"Shhh it's fine. I am helping you," Max said, but as he looked at Leslie's sexy thigh and panties, that "want" in him began to take over. He pulled her dress over her head and laid it on the chair near the bed. Then, he began to massage her shoulders. Max let his fingers spread over her back as he felt her respond with deep sighs. The massage did help Leslie recover and then she realized she was on a bed, her dress was off, and a very sexy boy was touching her body.

Just then, Max released her bra, which fell to the bed before she could catch it. Leslie felt his hands come around to her stomach area and begin to caress her skin. His face drew close to her own, and she felt a kiss on her neck.

"Max I feel better now..." she tried to object, but his hands were moving up her middle toward her naked breasts. He was seductively kissing her neck down to her shoulder where he began to kiss and suck her. When his fingers closed over her small breasts fondling and squeezing them, Leslie felt surges of desire and panic. "Max no..." she gasped. "This is wrong." But she did not try to stop the wonderful feelings he was giving her.

He lowered her to the bed and pulled his shirt off. He was a perfect specimen of muscle and flesh, and the sight of his sexy upper body made Leslie gasp. Then, he pulled her to him and kissed her mouth deeply. His tongue penetrated her lips immediately and Leslie responded without thinking by sucking his tongue and licking his mouth. She felt his hand slide along her thigh to the crotch of her panties.

"Max please..." Leslie complained weakly. "I am married." Max felt the wet between her legs so he knew she wanted to be fucked.

"He isn't here and you are mine now," he said, unbuckling his pants. He stood up and pulled his pants and shorts down revealing his long and thick cock that was rock hard and ready to fuck her. Leslie gasped at the size. It was easily twice the size of her husband in length and thickness. Her eyes were glued to it.

Max sat down next to her and kissed her shoulder, biting it again. He took her fingers and wrapped them around that big hard penis. "It is bigger than his, isn't it?" He moaned into her ear.

"Yes," was all she could answer.

"I am sexier than him, aren't I?" he asked, squeezing her left tit hard and pinching her nipple.

"Oh god yes," was all she could say. He was so strong and forceful and he was taking her with pure lust, like she hadn't felt from Robert in years. He pulled her mouth to his, kissed her, and lowered her to the bed, climbing on top of her. Forcefully, he turned her over and pulled her naked ass up toward his hard cock. He knelt behind her and pushed her thighs open and then grabbed her ass cheeks and parted them too.

Leslie was on fire inside but also in a panic. She had never fucked any guy other than Robert, and Max's cock was so big she was afraid it would rip her open inside. Firmly, Max pulled Leslie's pussy his way and parted the lips so he saw the pink vagina hole of another man's wife. He leaned in and fit his cock head to that hole, and leaned over her, pulling her to her hands and knees. He bit her back and pushed.

Leslie tried to scream as that huge cock spread her pussy rim and stretched her insides as each inch pushed up inside her. Instead of a scream, a deep sexual moan came out. The massive cock pushed deeper and deeper until it hit her cervix. It filled parts of her womb that had never felt a cock, taking that part of her virginity.

His thrusts were deep and strong, fucking in and out of her. Leslie felt his hands on her breasts squeezing and pinching them, and he kissed and bit her, moaning as he fucked inside her. "You want this. You want me to fuck you hard," he said in almost an animal-like growl.

"Yes!" she found herself saying.

"Say it!" he insisted. Leslie felt like she could not refuse him anything.

"Fuck me. I want it. Fuck me hard," she gasped, ashamed that her good wife mouth said those things to this huge sexy boy who was inside her. As she said that, his thrusts got faster and faster. Leslie was moaning and wiggling under his huge body. "Pull out. Don't cum in me," she begged. But just then her orgasm hit like a tornado and so did his. He pushed her flat and shot a huge load of hot cum deep in her womb.

Leslie came so hard she lost touch with the world for a while. When she came to, she heard the door open.

"Oh my god Leslie!" she heard Amber say and the girl quickly shut the door. "Where's Max?"

"I don't know!" Leslie said weakly as Amber helped her sit up. There was a second door from the bedroom that went out to a balcony, and it was open. Max was gone. Amber just held her friend and comforted her. "Please don't tell anyone," Leslie begged her friend.

Amber just kissed Leslie's lips and eased her into bed whispering, "Don't worry. We have lots of secrets." Saying that, Amber slipped out of her skirt and top, got under covers with her the sexy youth leader's wife, and gave her all of the comfort she needed...and then some.

5 BEFORE WE DIE

Steven, Lisa, and Rebecca knew each other well from their many ski outings over the years. At the lodge before the last day of their trip, Steven made it a point to talk to both Lisa and Rebecca, who always stayed side by side as they were great friends from way back in middle school. Now with the busy lives of college students, these ski trips five or six times a winter were also a reunion of people who rarely saw each other because of busy lives.

Lisa was a lovely strawberry blond girl with a short haircut that worked well for her when she skied. She was the shorter of the two girls, which was easy because Rebecca was quite tall with a slender figure that would have made her a great model if she didn't already have a career picked out to be a veterinarian after college. When Steven went for more beverages, both girls giggled.

"I forgot how cute he is!" Lisa laughed.

"Definitely," Rebecca agreed. "Dibs, I'm going to ski with him tomorrow."

"Dibs back at ya girl," Lisa teased her friend. "I'll beat you to him so watch your ass."

"Maybe we'll just share him!" Rebecca giggled, and that idea turned both girls into teenagers for a minute. The wine didn't hurt with that transformation.

As the party wound down, Steven made his way back to his room thinking about the many beautiful girls he could flirt with while skiing the next day. Just as he turned the corner to the hall where his room was, he stopped in his tracks. She saw him just as he spotted her. It was his old fiancée, Amber.

"Well hello, Steven," Amber said with a blush. "I didn't notice that you were in this group."

Steven approached her cautiously. "I am as surprised as you are, Amber," he said, trying to be as nice as he could. The relationship had ended badly and a lot of hurtful things were said. Still, she looked amazing as always, wearing a tight fitting tube top and a black skirt that showed her very pale thighs.

Steven failed to keep himself from checking her out and part of that was the drinks he had consumed at the party. She unlocked her door and stared at him seductively. The relationship ended for many ugly reasons, but good sex was not the problem. "You are glad to see me, aren't you butt boy?" she asked, using a nickname he didn't want anyone to know.

"Well…" he started to say and she pushed the door open, pulling him by his hand toward the bed.

"You want to come in. I know you want in," she said pulling him toward the bed.

"No Amber, I do not want to be in your room," he objected.

"I didn't mean the room," she said and she pulled him on top of her on the bed, kissing him deeply.

As much as Steven had sworn off his deviant ex lover, his erection sprang to life and pressed against her stomach. Just then, Steven realized the door was open and tried to bolt to close it so the others in the party would not see and have that ruin his chance with great girls, like Lisa and Rebecca.

Steven realized the only way out of this situation would be to fuck his way out. He knelt on the bed, unzipped his pants, and pulled out his long hard cock. As soon as Amber saw it, she gasped and began to breathe hard. Steven fell on top of Amber and forcefully started to pull up her skirt.

"Oh god! Yes, fuck me!" she moaned and he winced at her talk for fear someone would hear. He reached in and yanked her thong from her pussy and pulled it free, letting it fall to the floor. With an expertise that comes from fucking Amber many times, Steven held her hips and let his hard-on find her wet pussy.

His full shaft buried into her wet insides in one thrust and Steven started to fuck her. He knew a gentle fuck was not for her so he hooked his arms around her legs and rolled her back so her cunt would be angled up for a solid fucking. Steven grunted and he thrust in and out of her, hoping to end it fast. But just then she skillfully swiveled her hips and his cock fell out all wet from her pussy juices.

Amber kept her legs pulled back and reached down and grasped the shaft of Steven's hard cock.

"Not in that hole, lover. You know what you want," she said, and Steven remembered why she called him butt boy. Obediently he leaned in and let her fit the head of his cock in her anal opening. His cock was plenty wet with pussy juices, and Amber rotated her butt to help the head force open her tight butthole.

His cock pushed up her fast in a sudden surge that took it halfway inside her.

"Oh god, Steven! Fuck my ass," she gasped, pushing back as her fingers reached between them to find her clit.

The deviancy of it all got to Steven in a hurry and so he only had to thrust in and out of her butt a few times when he shot his load in that hole. Amber moaned and had her orgasm within seconds after she felt his hot cum fill her anal tunnel.

Amber slumped back and pulled Steven toward her to kiss. But he was driven to get out of there. He pulled himself together and made his escape as Amber watched, planning how she would get him to fuck her on the mountain the next day.

When the World Changed

The next morning at breakfast, Steven did not see Amber, and that was a relief. He sat at a big table with a lot of people and enjoyed the normalcy of it all. Rebecca and Lisa were both there but not sitting together. While they were having a ball flirting with all of the guys in the group, both of them stopped and waved at Steven as he sat down to eat. He liked that.

That day on the slopes was a good one. At one point, he was able to ride the lift up to the top with Rebecca, and you could cut the flirting tension with a knife. As soon as they got off, Lisa swooshed up and joined him on his trip down. It was a fun competition that was good-natured and made the day even more fun than it already was.

Around 4 p.m., the management began to hold anyone from going down the slopes until everyone was off the lifts. Steven found himself standing near Lisa and Rebecca. There was a lot of confusion until suddenly a rumble came from higher up the mountain.

"Folks we need to clear the mountain," someone in authority announced over the loud speaker. "We have received a word of an avalanche watch and that rumble we all just heard confirms it. We all need to get down the fastest way possible and that way is to ski down. So please everyone ski safely to the bottom and go to the vans so we can get away from this mountain. Now go."

Steven was one of the first out of the gate and he was a very fast skier. The idea of being taken in a snow-slide put fire in his legs and he was flying like the wind. Only a few were keeping up with him. He looked back and the closest ones were Lisa and Rebecca, and further back was a small army of skiers. He spotted Amber in that crowd.

Suddenly what seemed like a roar of an earthquake went off rumbling the ground and making a huge commotion. Steven looked back and he was horrified to see a mammoth wall of snow plummeting down that mountain ready to overtake everyone in their group.

"HURRY!" he shouted back, looking frantically for a route to safety that he could take quickly. Then he spotted it. There was a cabin at the base of a growth of trees. It was all he had. He turned suddenly and looked back to the girls. "FOLLOW ME!" he shouted, and they did. All three of the young skiers flew toward that cabin. They reached it just in time as Steven pushed the door open and threw their equipment inside.

Just then, the avalanche overtook the rest of the skiers. Screams could barely be heard over the rumble. Steven looked up and saw Amber get swallowed up by the snow. He pushed Lisa and Rebecca ahead of him and then he dived in and pushed the door shut just as the wall of snow hit the cabin.

Are We Dead?

The snow rammed into the building, making it moan and shake. Steven fell to the floor pulling the girls under him. His instinct to protect them kicked in. Lisa and Rebecca held on to Steven as the building shook as if it might fall in on them. Just then, it became completely dark as the snow covered the windows. And then it was still.

"Are we dead?" Lisa said softly. All three could hear their hearts beating fast.

"No," Steven said trying to look around, but it was pitch black in the middle of the day. Suddenly Steven realized that he had his arm wrapped around Rebecca's front to pull her to him, and his fingers were grasping her left breast tightly. His other hand had found its way over Lisa's back and the fingers were grasping the left cheek of her ass. In his mind, he remembered the nickname that Amber had for him – butt man. He also thought of that horrible image of Amber being swallowed by the rushing avalanche and that it almost certainly meant that everybody on that mountain was dead.

Soon the tremors died down and the three of them laid on the floor holding each other and shaking in fear. Both girls were softly weeping, so Steven stroked their hair and held them to him. He took inventory. It was dark but not as dark as when the avalanche was pounding them. He saw that the snow was over almost the entire window, but there were small segments of light that came through so they could begin to see.

Steven assessed that the building had withstood the impact and was showing no sign of falling on them. He remembered just as they dove into the door of the cabin that there were trees between the cabin and the fast moving snow and behind it, and he thought maybe those trees took a lot of the force of the impact. That was the good news.

The bad news is they were cut off. There was no escape from that cabin. Air was coming in through cracks in the windows and the chimney, but they could not get out. With the avalanche killing dozens of skiers, it might be days or longer before anyone checked that cabin.

"I am going to check things out," Steven whispered.

"No Steven, please!" Lisa pleaded hysterically and she began to weep which set Rebecca off crying as well. Steven only knew one thing to do. He kissed her. It was a deep and soulful kiss and became wet with tongues being exchanged. Rebecca pulled in close and began to kiss Steven on the cheek and ear. Then he kissed her, too. His tongue slid into her mouth and she sucked it as Lisa sucked his neck.

It seemed impossible considering they were snowbound, wet, and terrified that he really wanted to fuck them both right then. He could tell by their kisses that they were ready and that the sweet intimacy of having him inside their vaginas would be comforting to them. Finally, Steven held both of their heads and petted their hair to slow things down.

"Girls, I think we are ok for now. Let me see if I can get light so we can figure out what to do."

"I am so glad you are with us, Steven," Rebecca said.

"What would we do without you?" Lisa said, their hands stroking his face, hair, neck, and shoulders.

With plenty of assurances and talking to the girls all the while, Steven did find provisions in the cabin. There was food and he found some lanterns and matches and got them going. The cabin had several bedrooms with comfortable looking beds. One entire bedroom even had firewood kept inside so it would be dry. The stove did not have power but there were camping stoves and plenty of canisters of fuel to run them.

The girls responded with glee to his finds. Soon Lisa was cooking up a nice meal while Rebecca and Steven turned their little refugee camp into a home. There was joy in their friendship and that they were alive when many dear friends just outside that snowed-in door were not. As Steven was talking to Lisa about their prospects, suddenly Rebecca came out of one of the bedrooms wearing a pretty dress.

"I found clothes!" she said with a giggle and both Lisa and Steven laughed and clapped their hands at how pretty she looked. The cabin must have belonged to a family because there were lots of cute things for the girls to wear. After they ate, Steven was treated to a fashion show, and as each girl walked out in another cute skirt or dress, they let their hero get an eyeful of leg, panties, or down their front at their pretty boobs.

As it grew dark, the reality of their situation set in. The three friends sat cuddled together in front of the fire. They had thought they would each go to a bedroom where there were lots of blankets to keep warm. Just then, in the flickering light of the fire, Steven saw tears on Lisa's face.

"What's wrong beautiful?" he asked softly as Rebecca rested her head on his shoulder.

"I don't want to sleep apart," she said, taking his hand and holding it in both of hers. "Can't we all sleep together? If this is our last night to be alive, I want to give anything to you. Before we die, let's at least have one last time to know love."

Rebecca hugged her friend as Steven began to understand what Lisa meant. As he got up to get the bedding pulled into the living room in front of the fire, he looked back and saw Lisa and Rebecca kiss each other's lips for the first time.

Our Last Night on Earth

Steven took off the pajama shirt that he had on. All three of the stranded skiers had found something fun to wear to bed, and the girls looked cute in their skimpy nighties that they picked out. They arranged the mattresses on the floor with lots of pillows and blankets from the bedrooms, and Steven added big logs of wood to the fire so the room would stay warm for a long time. It would not just be warm, he thought to himself, it might become very hot in more ways than one.

He went to the kitchen area and got some water that they had made with melted snow, and as he looked to the huge makeshift bed, he saw the gorgeous girls he had all to himself snuggling, whispering, and exchanging tiny kisses. When Steven came in both girls gasped at the curves of his well-developed chest. Steve himself was getting an eyeful of Rebecca's long legs that were on full display in her skimpy nightie.

"You girls should not tempt your old ski buddy by looking that sexy," he said softly with a teasing smile.

Lisa crawled to him on her hands and knees and took his hand, pulling him to bed. "Come in here big boy so we can tempt you some more. Before we die, we want pleasure," she said in her best sexy nymph voice, but Steven was hypnotized by the view down her blouse, at the shape of her gorgeous breasts, with just the hint of nipple trying to peek out.

Steven laughed and let Lisa pull him down onto the huge makeshift bed of mattresses, blankets, pillows, and girls. He fell onto his back, pulled Lisa to him, and kissed her mouth deeply. Any tiny bit of charade that they would ever go back to being just three friends disappeared when that kiss became very passionate. He felt Lisa's tongue slip into his mouth and he began to suck it while his own tongue licked her lips.

That charade also vanished as Steven felt his pants begin to be opened by the sweet slender fingers of the beautiful Rebecca. Steven looked away from that sexy wet kiss Lisa was giving him, and she did not hesitate to kiss along his jaw to his neck and start to suck it passionately. He looked down to see Rebecca pulling down his pants and his shorts until his rock hard penis popped out into view. She finished the job of stripping the hero who saved the lives of his two lovers.

Rebecca smiled with delight seeing that this sexy hero was so turned on. She slid her hands up his thighs on her hands and knees, swaying her sexy butt back and forth as she stalked that hard cock. She made eye contact with him and licked her lips, then lowered her round lips to it and let it slide into her mouth.

"Oh god!" he moaned with pleasure, letting his hand stroke Rebecca's soft hair as she pleasured his hard cock inside her mouth, riding up and down on it with her lips and tongue. Lisa saw what Rebecca had in her mouth and kissed her way down Steven's body to enjoy a taste of his hard cock herself. As she moved, her sexy thighs passed by Steven's face and he pulled them to him and began to kiss her legs.

Lisa gasped and threw her hair back as

she glanced back and saw that Steve was lowering her hips to his face to taste her pussy. He found that wet cunt, lapped at her slit, and began to suck her clit just as she started licking the head of his cock. Rebecca yielded that head so she could lick Steve's sexy balls.

Steven always dreamed of a three way, but the idea that he was rolling around in front of a romantic fire with two of his good friends who were on fire to suck and fuck him was a dream. All three forgot the danger they were in and gave in to every passion. There were so many things that neither had tried that now excited them tremendously. As they both licked the head of Steve's cock, their lips met and a deep wet kiss developed around the wet skin of his erection.

"Oh god, Rebecca! This is amazing!" Lisa whispered, knowing that Rebecca also had never kissed or had sex with a girl.

Rebecca was full of lust for Lisa's mouth, and when she kissed her again, they rolled off of Steve and began to make out on the bed as Steve looked at those sexy bodies making love. He crawled toward them and looked between those four sexy thighs at the round pussies ready to be fucked.

His cock was aching to get inside either girl, so when he saw Lisa roll on top of Rebecca with both of their legs wide open, it was a pussy stacked on a pussy grinding together. Steve laid between that temple of sex of their sexy thighs and began to lick from Lisa's cute butt down along her sweet pink pussy slit, loving her clit and then right on through to Rebecca's clit and down to her vagina opening in one sweet sexy lick.

Lisa was on fire feeling Steve licking her cunt as she and Rebecca made out with a passion that seemed to double by the minute. Rebecca pushed up for air and Lisa let her mouth move to her sweet little sexy tits.

Rebecca moaned, "Oh yes Lisa, yes," as she felt her left nipple slide into her best friends mouth.

Lisa liked the nipple and sucked it eagerly, pulling it deeper as she pushed her clit up into Rebecca's pussy on top of her, grinding on her cunt. Suddenly Lisa gasped because she could feel Steve getting into position. When his hard cock slid into her vagina, the rim spread open to let him fuck her as deep as he could.

As Steve fucked Lisa's wet hole steadily, trying to take it easy and not come too fast, he fell on Rebecca and kissed and bit up and down her soft back. Steve's lust for both girls was out of control because as he fucked Lisa and tasted Rebecca, his hands were around her middle and finding their way to stroke and squeeze Lisa's round tits under her friend. But then he had to have Rebecca too, so he slid his cock out of Lisa, moved it up a few inches and plunged into the cunt of the slim and sexy Rebecca all the way to the balls.

The cries of excitement and pleasure filled the cabin as the girls wiggled on top of each other getting fucked at the same time by the same amazing guy. Steve was out of his mind feeling his cock plunge into each wet hole and the warm pussy of Lisa pull him inside her only to then fill up Rebecca's oozing hole as well. Suddenly his orgasm hit and he shot inside of Rebecca. The first wave made him double over her as she leaned around and kissed him deeply.

As soon as the first surges of his orgasm passed, Steve pulled out of Rebecca and plunged his hard cock into Lisa's pussy. Then the second wave hit and he came in her too. Just then both girls orgasmed within moments of each other, pressing their breasts down on each other and moaning, kissing, and gasping for air.

Rebecca rolled off of Lisa and gasped for air. Steve fell onto the bodies of these two amazing girls and moaned.

"Oh my god! That was amazing!" he said.

Then the giggles hit when the three lovers realized how many taboos they had all crossed together.

"If I die now, this will make it worth it," Steve said with a happy laugh, pulling Rebecca back to him and kissing her neck.

Lisa leaned in and kissed Steve and then her best friend, and their loving kisses seemed to go on as time stood still. Even though Steve had just shot a huge load inside of two sexy girls, he grew hard again. When Rebecca felt it, she rolled over and spread her legs, and reached out to him.

"Fuck me," she said, amazed how slutty she was for this man.

"No, fuck me," Lisa added, reaching down and grasping his hard cock while she kissed

Steve's lips.

The three sweethearts fucked all night. At times, they fell in a pile and when Steve woke up, he was inside a girl but not sure which one. They fucked so many times that none of them could count it and by morning, they were a heap of naked flesh, cum, and sweat.

Rescuers

Mr. Hartunian and Mr. Reaves had the grim task of finding the bodies after one of the worst avalanches to hit these ski slopes in a century. It was hard to figure out how many were buried because the avalanche hit so fast and was so destructive that it swept away the ski lift, the workers, and all of the skiers it seemed. The closest they could tell there were dozens killed. The two worked tirelessly down the mountain, searching for those who were making any sound to rescue the living before retrieving the dead.

"Hey Lou, we got help," Mr. Reaves said to Mr. Hartunian. They both spotted Leo and Fred from the lodge digging kids out, and the ambulance was parked at the top of the mountain. Other men were setting up ropes with stretchers to pull the survivors to safety. Just then, Mr. Reaves spotted something. They both figured it out together that the smoke rising up from the trees below was coming from a building.

"That's the Spencer cabin. They are

usually not in it this time of year," Mr. Reaves said.

As the two rescuers approached the cabin on their skis, they saw that it was almost completely buried in the avalanche snow. But it was standing and smoke was billowing out of the chimney. The men got to the cabin and worked towards a window where there was a small part of the top that revealed light coming from inside.

Mr. Hartunian reached the window and gazed inside. "Well Stan, do you see anyone in there? Are they dead?"

What Stan saw was far from a death scene. In the middle of the floor of the living room was a boy and two very sexy girls laying together naked. They were asleep, but every few moments one would move toward the other and deliver a kiss.

"No, Mr. Reaves," Mr. Hartunian answered. "We can go back to people that really need our help. I don't think these kids even want to be rescued."

6 LIFELONG FRIENDS

Keeping In Touch

"**O**h my god. No way!" Erin giggled laying in her bed in her college dorm room as she talked on her cell phone. These calls were her lifeline because she missed her best friend from high school so much. So when Erin made contact with Susan each night using her cell phone, that let them chatter away like they did growing up together. "Where were you?" Erin asked, laughing at the situation she was hearing about.

"It was an end of year mixer thrown by Professor Duncan and his wife Teena. Oh my god, Erin, you should see these two. They should quit teaching and model," Susan laughed.

"I bet all the boys at the mixer had hard-ons for her," Erin added.

"Oh they did, and she was teasing them

like a real slut. But the more she got those guys horny, the more excited her husband got. It was at this room in the student center, so there were a lot of back rooms. There were other teachers and chaperones there too. So I was in the kitchen refilling the tea when I saw the professor and his hot wife slipping back to one of those rooms."

"Oh my god, Susan! Were they going to fuck right there at the college mixer?" Erin squealed.

"They so did!" Erin's best friend answered with delight. "And get this, I found a spot to watch it all!"

"Shut up!" Erin laughed so hard that the other girls in the dorm heard it.

"No, you shut up!" Susan giggled. "It was so hot to watch, Erin. It was this big room that was used for events, but that night it was mostly being used for storage. I had gone back in there to put up some extra punch bowls in a closet at the back of the room. I saw them sneak in there, and he started kissing her really hard and feeling up her tits even before the door was closed."

Both girls were gasping at the picture that Susan was painting. Erin did not say a word, but she slipped out of her shorts and into her bed. She was glad her roommate was on a date so she could listen to Susan telling about what she saw.

"He was talking so dirty, Erin," Susan continued. "He said things like 'I wanted to fuck you right in front of those collage kids.' And she said things back like 'every girl in there wants my husband's big hard cock'."

"How could you stand it, Susan?" Erin said breathing heavier. She didn't dare tell her best friend from childhood that she has slipped her hand into her panties and begun to touch her clit imagining this story.

"I was going crazy, Erin!" Susan answered. From there Susan went on to describe how the professor and Teena found a spot in that storage room so that Teena could unzip his pants and pull out the professor's very large hard cock. His wife sucked her husband eagerly as the party went on just a few yards away. Then the professor stood up with his cock waving away out of his pants and bent her over an unused ping-pong table.

From where Susan was hiding, she could see Teena's wet pussy and the opening to her vagina when her husband spread it with his fingers so he could penetrate her right there as she bent for him. She watched that big cock drive inside the young wife as the professor started fucking her hard and fast.

By this time, Erin was masturbating actively and trying all she could not to let on to her best friend Susan. After all, Susan and she had gone through confirmation together at the Methodist church where they both attended. But Erin did not know that on the other end Susan had her hand under her skirt so she could stroke her clit as she talked to Erin as well.

"Erin, I could tell when he shot in her," Susan finished. "He suddenly stiffened up and grabbed her naked ass and buried that big cock in her and moaned. His butt cheeks were flexing like crazy, so I could tell he was emptying his cum inside his wife as I watched. It just kept going as he shot and shot and shot."

Erin stroked her clit. "And shot and shot...," she repeated in a far away tone. She felt her orgasm coming along, and that force inside her was taking over.

"In...side...her...," Susan gasped as she slid her wet finger from the rim of her oozing pussy hole to her clit faster and fast.

"Oh god, oh god, oh god...," Erin moaned and then she gurgled into the phone. Her orgasm surged through her making her wiggle on the bed, sliding her finger deep into her wet vagina. Susan reached her peak almost exactly at the same time, describing that professor fuck his wife almost in public made Susan come while talking on the phone with her best friend in the world. Then she just slumped back to whisper and giggle with Erin for hours.

Summer Break at Last

Erin and Susan hated being apart all year. Since first grade, they had been inseparable. Their moms were the best of friends, and their dads bowled and went fishing together. Both of the girls were "only" children, so they filled the role of sisters as much as they did best friends. When they graduated high school, they celebrated at each other's houses, and each girl got as many presents from the other parents as from their own.

As much as the BFFs wanted to go to college together and be roommates, it was not possible with the scholarships they got and their degree goals. Susan went to state school, while Erin attended a private Christian school that was 100 miles away. At first that 100 miles seemed like a galaxy far far away, but they learned to stay close with daily phone calls.

Summer arrived and Erin and Susan could not be happier. With successful freshman years behind them, the summer gave them time to be together and live at home like when they were kids. Those first reunions were so loud with the giggling, squealing, and dancing that Erin's dad had to put his hands over his ears and finally leave the room.

The dads and moms had to get used to all that joyful friendship for the summer because the separation made the girls even closer. They commonly walked in the park holding hands. The second weekend of the summer, they were sitting on a picnic blanket at the park and holding hands and sharing every detail they experienced at school.

Just then, two ten-year-old boys came racing along on their bikes dodging between people who were having picnics or just walking in the park. But what one of the boys yelled out was impossible to miss.

"Dykes!" he yelled to the two girls, and then they raced on so they would not get in trouble. As soon as the girls heard what the boy said, they burst out in a gale of laughter.

"Oh my god, that is so dumb!" Erin roared.

"Stupid kids!" Susan added and they enjoyed that good laugh. But when Erin slipped her hand back into hers, Susan felt that sense of joy and completeness that no other friend could do except this one girl that she loved above all others. Erin held her best friend's hand and thought about it. There was no question she loved Susan deeply. But that line of loving each other romantically was not one that had ever been crossed.

Both girls were one hundred percent boy crazy. That evening, Erin dropped her friend off at the door. Standing by her car, they hugged.

"I just missed you so much," Susan said, hugging her lifelong friend tightly. Erin petted the hair of this girl she loved so much. Susan looked up and there were tears of joy in her eyes.

Just then, Erin did something that surprised her. She gently kissed Susan's lips. Even more of a revelation was that Susan kissed her back. When they kissed, the girls stared at each other with eyes wide with the realization of what just happened. Then Susan giggled to break the tension.

"Ok fine, I am a dyke," Erin said jokingly. "But I am your dyke," she teased and with that she kissed her friend on the mouth quickly and slipped away doing a little dance to the driver's side of the car.

"Bye-bye dyke," Susan said with childlike playfulness. "I love you so much!"

Going To the Go-Go

The girls decided to meet for lunch at the sandwich shop to plan their day. Erin got there early and ordered her usual half of a turkey sandwich on rye. When Susan showed up, it was clear she was very excited. She ordered a salad and then pulled way over into the booth and whispered, "I have something to show you. Slide over here with me."

Erin slid out of her side of the booth and in with her BFF toward the wall so they had some privacy. When they had made their order, Susan slipped her hand to her big purse and pulled out a copy of poster that she had torn down from a restaurant window near downtown. It was for a nightclub. Erin looked closer and then she gasped. The name of the club was Club Pussy. Erin looked at her friend in shock. "Oh my god, Susan! Is this a..."

"It's a lesbian bar!" she said with a giggle. Both of the girls giggled so much that people in the next booth thought it was two middle school girls. Quickly, Susan put the flyer away before their food came. Both girls started their lunches, but that flyer was on both of their minds. Suddenly, Susan just blurted it out. "I think we should go!" she said with a nervous laugh.

"No way!" Erin yelped. But the more the two girls giggled about it, the more the temptation to go somewhere so naughty seemed like an adventure they could not give up. They agreed to hit Club Pussy that next Friday night.

The days leading up to their big night of going to the Go-Go for lesbians were all about preparation. That preparation included finding just the right sexy outfits. But they also talked a lot about how to behave. They decided to do all they could to send out the vibe that they were together. They were there to watch the show of lesbians in their natural habitat and not to get picked up. Giving off that vibe would call for a certain amount of dancing together, kissing, and holding hands, but the girls were so at ease with each other, that seemed harmless enough for a big night of adventure.

The girls looked amazing as they stepped out of the cab at the Club Pussy. But moments later when they stepped into the explosive environment of the lesbian bar, it was the girls that stood in stunned shock. The sight of a dance floor full of sexy women pushing against each other, dancing, kissing, and pulling their bodies close was even more than either girl had expected.

Quickly, Susan grabbed Erin's hand and pulled her to the dance floor. Erin seemed in a daze, so Susan pulled her body to her and ground up and down on it. Erin looked at her best friend oozing all over her and just mouthed, "Oh my god, Susan!" because it was too loud to talk. Susan was watching the other girls around her to try to fit in. She swallowed hard watching a tall exotic looking girl lean in and kiss her partner full on the mouth. They began to make out, sliding tongues together. Susan nudged Erin to see what she was seeing.

When Erin looked back at her friend, Susan made a gesture by putting her finger to her own lips and then to Erin's. The message was clear that Susan knew they had to kiss like that or they would not fit in. Shyly Erin nodded and moved closer to her friend. The wild action of lesbians kissing and feeling each other erased all nervousness.

Just then, Susan was bumped from behind, and that force forced her forward to kiss Erin. Erin felt Susan's lips on her and gave in to the moment. She brought her her arms up and pressed against her back kissing her deeply and letting her mouth open. She felt the squeal that Susan put up inside her mouth more than heard it. Then Susan pulled Erin's head to her and kissed back pushing her tongue into her lips.

As they gasped and stopped for a minute, they could tell many of the lesbians dancing around them were watching. So Susan leaned in and kissed her best friend again, but this time with sloppy open-lipped kisses. Her tongue licked Erin's mouth, dipping inside only briefly. At first, Erin was in shock trying to keep pace, but then she understood that this was a show of passion for the benefit of the lesbians. She began to kiss and lick Susan's mouth feeling her tongue slip inside Susan's lips as she began to suck it. Inside both girls were having fun playing the lesbian game but at the same time hiding that they were very turned on.

The next dance was a fast one, so the girls used their best moves to shake their bottoms and be sexy for each other and for the show of all. It was during this dance that suddenly Erin turned and found herself dancing with a gorgeous, tall dark-skinned woman. She looked over and Susan was having lots of fun dancing with a very pale and skinny girl with a cute short dress on. The flirting was nonstop and lots of fun.

But when that beautiful vixen that Erin was dancing with pulled Erin close and planted her hands on her butt cheeks, Erin got uncomfortable. The woman was amazingly hot and aggressive. She put her hand in Erin's hair and then pulled her head back and kissed her with a deep sexual kiss. Erin felt the woman's tongue thrust into her mouth in and out simulating a fucking motion. Erin was at the same time frightened and so turned on by being "taken" like this. When the kiss broke, the woman whispered into Erin's ear. "Are you taken? Because I want to fuck you."

Erin looked into the woman's deep brown eyes and felt tempted in a way she had never felt before. She was trying to remember how to talk when she felt her fingers twine into the finger of her sweet friend Susan. She looked over and Susan pulled her away from the aggressive lesbian and kissed her. As the girls scooted way, Erin looked back at the woman, smiled, and mouthed at the woman "taken."

There were lots of little rooms off of the big dance floor where it was quieter. The girls began to explore and found a place to sit together at a bar and have a couple glasses of wine. "This place is crazy, but it's hot!" Susan said, sipping her wine.

"You saved me!" Erin said, giggling. "That woman wanted to fuck me."

"Who wouldn't?" Susan said, teasing her sexy friend. The wine helped the girls settle down so they had several glasses. They did not feel out of place as much, and they were having a big adventure. The raw sex between the dozens of sexy women was out in the open. It was hard not to stare. The booths were made with wide couch benches to make it easy to lie down. To the right two women were kissing deeply. One of them with long black hair unzipped her lover's dress, pulled it down in front, and began to fondle and then suck her naked breasts without shame.

"Oh my, god! Look in that room." Erin whispered. Through a door, two naked women were rolling around on top of a table. One of the women had something strapped to her hips that held a large plastic cock. She pushed the slender girl with very short hair, so she was facing up and then the black haired woman opened her legs and moved that big cock between her legs.

Suddenly, the short-haired girl gasped as her lover penetrated her pussy with that big dildo. Kissing her passionately, the girl on top began to fuck her like a man would do.

That was when Susan whispered into Erin's ear softly, "Its time to go." Erin agreed and they calmly made their way out to the street to find a cab to take them home.

Oh What A Night

The girls had to be quiet going into Susan's house, so they did not wake her parents. "Do you need to call or go home or anything?" Susan whispered.

"No," Erin answered. "They know I am with you, so I am safe."

"I am not so sure how safe you are," Susan said with a giggle. It was an old joke they shared but tonight it took on new meaning. The girls had slept over at each other's houses so much that they kept nighties there so they didn't ever have to pack. "Do you want to stay over?" Susan asked.

"I better. It's like 2 a.m. and I feel a little tipsy," Erin answered, finding her nightie that she wore when she stayed with her best friend.

Susan checked on her parents, and they were sound asleep so she and her lifelong friend settled in on the couch to talk about all they had experienced at Club Pussy. The girls had to suppress their giggling at what they saw, but almost without thinking, they began to cuddle pulling several throw blankets over their legs and holding each other close.

The giggles died down, and as they lay there together quietly, Erin felt her heart rate getting faster just being in an embrace with Susan. Susan felt the same thing. Finally, Erin said softly, "What was the most exciting thing about tonight?"

There was a pause, and then Susan said slowly so it came out right, "The most exciting part was being there with you."

Erin looked into the eyes of her best friend and touched her face tenderly. Susan was almost lying on Erin as they reclined on the couch. Then as though drawn in, Erin kissed her lips.

The kisses at the club were a mixture of play and passion. Now in the quiet of that dark living room with the girls all alone, the kisses were a mixture of passion and love. Those hot wet kisses on the dance floor stayed with both Erin and Susan. Now with the entire night to themselves, those deep kisses came back as the girls opened their lips and let their tongues explore each other. Erin felt her dear friend's tongue lick her lips as they kissed, and then enter her mouth to probe that warm and wet place. Without thinking, Erin began to suck her tongue softly, drawing on it, which sent Susan into a passionate orbit of wanting more and more of Erin.

"I can't explain it, Erin, I just have this want inside for you that is so new," Susan gasped between kisses, letting her hands touch Erin's loose breasts inside her tiny nightie top.

Erin pulled the string on her top so it opened, letting her dear friend have access to her small boobs. Her nipples were hard and standing out because of how aroused she was for what they were doing.

"You are so sexy, Erin," Susan gasped looking at the exposed tits of her sweet friend. She sat up and pulled her nightie open, and her large breasts were exposed. Erin's eyes widened as she put her hands one on each tit and squeezed and fondled them.

Just then, there was a sound from the side of the house where Susan's parent's bedroom was.

"Oh no!" Susan gasped and both girls pulled her tops shut and scampered to Susan's bedroom. Susan pushed the door shut with the lights off and only the nightlight to see by. They were both terrified of being caught but also fighting off the giggles.

As Susan pressed her ear to the door and did not hear anything, she felt Erin slip her hands around her from behind Her fingers opened her top and found her ample boobs and began to squeeze them. Slowly the fingers drifted to her nipples caressing them as they became hard with excitement.

Susan leaned back into Erin moaning. "That is so hot Erin," she whispered, and she felt lips on her ears and neck kissing and sucking her skin.

Susan turned around and opened Erin's top again. Pressing her naked breasts into Erin's, she kissed her best friend deeply, pushing her toward her bed. As Erin fell back onto Susan's bed, she had to push away the army of stuffed animals that lived there since Susan was a little girl. Both girls giggled as Susan knelt on the floor next to the bed and pulled the shorts and panties of her best friend down her long slender legs.

"Yes, take me," Erin gasped as she pulled back on the bed and opened her legs wide like the girl at Club Pussy was doing for her lesbian lover. Susan kissed up Erin's legs and then looked down into the neatly trimmed pussy of her friend.

"I want you so much," she whispered. "I have never done this before. Tell me what you like." With that, Susan lowered her mouth to the folds of that pussy and started to kiss. Her curiosity is what pushed her passion for Erin's pussy as she parted the lips and began to lick the moist slit of her cunt.

Erin petted the hair of her friend as Susan explored her wide-open pussy. Erin felt Susan's tongue slide along her slit to her vagina and lap at the flow of wet that was coming from her insides. Then that tongue licked back up where Susan discovered the clit of her lifelong friend. Tenderly, she began to suck and lick it speeding up as she felt Erin begin to thrust and moan in passion.

"Oh god! Lick me out Susan. Suck my clit," Erin whispered, but she wanted to shout it out. But Susan was being creative because her fingers were squeezing Erin's thighs and sliding up and down her crack. Just then her index finger found her friend's hole and began to push inside to explore the deepest places of Erin's vagina. By this time, Erin was thrusting up to Susan's face and fucking her finger back as it moved in and out. Suddenly, Erin grabbed Buster the stuffed bear, buried her mouth in his fur, and moaned. Her orgasm hit hard, which drove Susan wild with licking and sucking her pussy.

As Susan crawled up on the bed, they were both gasping. Susan giggled and kissed Erin whispering, "I loved eating your pussy."

It made it even more exciting being such dirty girls right under the nose of Susan's parents. Erin did not answer, but she pushed her mouth onto Susan's, kissing it hard and pressing her down on to her own bed. Susan took Buster and laid him nearby for further use.

Erin turned and began kissing down Susan's body toward her sexy open thighs. The whiteness of her round thighs called to Erin to come and taste the joy of her best friend's pussy. When Erin looked down into that soft hair, the folds of Susan's pussy excited her tremendously. She quickly leaned in and used fingers from both hands to part the lips and look deeply into the pink slit, and at the sexy vagina and anal holes that were before her eyes.

For a brief second, Erin hesitated because she had never licked a pussy before, much less the pussy of her dearest friend. Her legs were near Susan's head so just then Susan reached up and slid her finger into Erin's wet hole. Erin gasped and gave in to the lust for Susan's body and began licking her cunt up and down just as Susan had done to her. Susan's moans were soft and throaty as her hips humped up and down each time Erin licked her stiff clit button.

Erin held Susan's butt cheeks firmly as she ate out her best friend, letting her mouth lick and suck every hidden part of Susan's pussy. When she licked down to her vagina hole, Erin even tried to enter it with her tongue. When Susan felt the tip of Erin's tongue go up into her vagina, her orgasm caused her whole body to convulse.

"Oh god, oh god, oh god, Erin, fuck me with your tongue!" just then Erin came again, and she lowered her hips to Susan's mouth. Susan's tongue pushed inside Erin's cunt when that orgasm surged through her body too. For seconds both girls writhed and thrust their cunts on to the face of the other in the ecstasy of mutual orgasms. Then they fell on the bed exhausted and feel asleep happily naked in each other's arms.

7 THE RING OF PASSION

A Man and His Fantasy

Like many people, Charles was a big fan of the Lord of the Rings. That concept of an ultimate ring that gave power to its wearer never ceased to fascinate him. Elaine was tolerant of her husband's fascination with the stories since she had known about it long before they got married. About two years after they got married, his fantasies about the stories got into their bedroom. She was just 27 years old and he was 31 years old, and their sex life had been struggling for almost a year.

Charles entered the bedroom with a long white robe on that she had never seen before. "I am Gandalf and I hold the magic ring!" he said commandingly. "You are helpless before its power, virgin maiden," he said with a goofy lofty voice.

Instead of awe, it caused Elaine to giggle like a schoolgirl, but that was better than the drudgery their sex life had been up until then. Charles held out his class ring on his finger, pointing it at her as if it really had power. There was no question that it gave him a new sexual energy in bed.

Charles stepped to the edge of the bed and Elaine stood up from her chair, fascinated by this sex game. With a wave of his arm, Charles commanded his slender wife, "You are my slave, you wench," and with that, he grabbed her hair, pulled her head back, and kissed her mouth roughly. When he finished, Charles threw his wife on the bed with all the power of a dark lord.

To the utter surprise of Charles, Elaine gasped "Oh God yes!" when he threw her down. His manly handling of her excited her, and she fell on her back, pulling her panties off. She had been a cold fish in bed, and becoming assertive turned her into a sex kitten. Charles ripped open his huge white Gandalf robe and his rock-hard cock was arching up toward his pretty wife's face.

"Oh God," Elaine gasped. In truth, she had never even seen it. In most of their sex, he just got on, stuck it in, shot, and got off. Seeing it made her even more out of control with passion.

Charles fell on his pretty wife with a new passion, roughly pulling her hair and sucking her neck. As his mouth sucked down to her shoulder, he bit her and that pain caused her to gasp and moan with pleasure. Elaine was on fire. She never knew how sexy it was to be dominated like this, but she loved this new rough sex her husband was trying out.

Charles roughly pushed his wife's sexy thighs apart to open her pussy for him to fuck. Throwing off the robe, he pushed up on one arm, with the other hand grabbed his throbbing cock, and moved it up and down her pink pussy slit. When it found the wet hole, he wedged the head into the rim and thrust it into her in one powerful lunge.

Elaine gasped and arched up to her husband. "Oh yes, fuck me, Master," she found herself saying.

Charles fucked in and out of his wife as if he were another creature. He held her ass cheeks and squeezed them hard, pounding into her warm vagina again and again and again. As Elaine moaned and suddenly came, Charles felt his balls begin to push his seed out. It exploded inside her, filling her with his cum.

Charles got up from the most amazing sex he had ever had with his wife and went to the bathroom to get a drink of water. He felt full of power and was amazed that Elaine let him dominate her like that. Maybe my class ring really did give me power, he thought to himself. As he entered the bedroom, Elaine just lay there like a freshly fucked woman. She was spread open and her sexy pussy was oozing his cum onto the sheet.

"Oh my God, Charles. That was amazing." She cooed like a woman freshly in love. Then Charlie made the mistake of trying to take it to the next level. He walked up and grabbed

Elaine, then flipped her over.

"Speak when spoken to, slave," he ordered, giving her a sharp slap on the ass. Then he parted her ass cheeks and started playing with her butthole.

That did not go well. Elaine jumped out of bed and went berserk with anger. She told her husband he was insane if he thought he could beat her or use her butt for sex and still expect anything from her. As fast as it all started, it was over and Charles was sleeping on the couch wondering what had gone wrong.

I Got To Get Rid Of This Ring

Charles had rented the Gandalf costume so after sleeping on the couch, he thought it was best to return it the next day. The costume shop had all kinds of oddities lying around that were more than just costumes. There were old lanterns, staffs, and other antiques of a time when magic ruled the world.

"How did that work out for you?" Mr. Masters asked as he took the costume back. Charles and Mr. Masters became friends when he got the costume and revealed what it was for to the owner of the store.

"OK, at first, Mr. Masters," Charles answered, "my wife got very turned on by the role-play. We went nuts and I fucked her brains out. But then when I went in for another time, she got mad. I went a little too far wanting to spank her and play with her butt," he said regretfully.

Then Charles looked down at this class ring that he used as part of his Gandalf role. "I guess this ring does not have infinite power over women after all," he said, handing the robes over to the costume store owner.

"Come with me for a minute, Charles. I think I have something for you that will help you out," Mr. Masters said, and he took Charles to a back room, which was not visible from the front of the store. Once the door was secured, he took a metal box out of a safe. He tapped it and said in a low voice, "This is a lead-lined box." Now Charles had his curiosity up.

Once Mr. Masters opened the box, he took out a smaller ring box. He held it in his hand, tapped it, and whispered, "Lead too." Then he opened it to reveal a shining silver ring. It had a pattern like a rope that wove around the outside and inside and had an inscription that was in another language. It looked very much like the image of the ring of power from the Tolkien books as it was shown in the movies.

"They call this the Ring of Passion," Mr. Masters said in a low voice. "I have to get rid of this ring. I cannot handle its power," he said in an ominous voice.

"How did you get it?" Charles asked, looking at the ring in awe.

"It has been handed down old man to young man for centuries. It was made by magicians in the middle ages right after the plague of the Black Death. Because Europe's population was almost wiped out, magicians made about two dozens of these to give to healthy young men so they could make any woman mate with them. It was made to repopulate the world. Now only a few are still around. I cannot keep it. I am too old for the amount of fucking it can give to you. If I keep it any longer, it will kill me," Mr. Masters said with regret in his voice.

The old owner of the Ring of Passion took the ring case out of the larger box and closed the smaller box. Then he pressed it onto Charles's palm. "Always carry it in the ring box. Do not even carry it close in your pocket. Its powers affect every female within line of sight. It has no effect on men or any other living thing. As soon as you take it out, any female near you will begin to go into a sexual frenzy. As best as I can tell, it affects the clitoris in some way."

Charles was stunned, but he closed his hand over that ring. "Any woman you use it on will be unable to stop herself from eagerly wanting to fuck you. It works through the instincts so the woman may cry out that she can't stop herself. If you did nothing, she would strip in front of you, try to get your cock out to suck you off, or just roll on the ground masturbating until she found relief in her own orgasm," Mr. Masters continued.

"That is amazing," Charles said, feeling his heart beating very fast at the prospect of what this ring could do for him.

"It has ultimate power over all human females. But you have to be careful on how you use it. Never use it on any female under 18 or the elderly. Don't even take a chance; it will affect those girls or women. They are not able to handle the intensity of the orgasms. You can kill someone with this thing," Mr. Masters said gravely.

"I promise to be careful," Charles promised.

"Also be careful not to take it out of its case or wear it where there will be crowds or girls or even more than one. There is nothing as frightening as seeing a roomful of women going wild with sexual need, and once you set it off, there is no stopping it. Even if you have a female lined up to fuck using the powers of the Ring of Passion, be 100% sure that no other females will enter the room while it is out. If you lose control of the situation, the danger to the girls or to you is huge," he continued.

"There is one last thing," he said. "If you need to get control over a situation, there is a swoon function. Simply point the ring at a woman and say in a firm tone, "Orgasm." When you do that, the woman will instantly have an overpowering orgasm. She will fall down and cum in huge waves and within moments, she will pass out or swoon. She will be out for a few minutes so you have time to escape."

A Little Demo

"This is all pretty amazing," Charles said,

holding the ring box in his hand. "Do you think you can show me how it works?"

"Just a moment." Mr. Masters opened the door to his back room and looked out into the store. There was just one customer in the store in the middle of the morning. Mr. Masters knew her, but he had never used the ring on her. Her name was Claire and she taught at the local middle school. Since it was summer session, she had time to browse strange little stores by herself. "OK, you go lock the front door so nobody comes in. Keep the ring in the box until I nod at you and then put it on," Mr. Masters said and then he stepped out into the store.

"Hello Mr. Masters," Claire said happily. She was a lovely woman in her early thirties with a slender waist and a substantial bust line. She always dressed nicely and today she was in an expensive skirt and blouse suit outfit because she was meeting with the school board later on.

"Hello Claire," Mr. Masters said in his warmest tone all the while watching Charles slip out and make his way to the front door. Claire paid Charles no mind because to her he was just another patron of the shop. "You look gorgeous today as always," Mr. Masters said smiling.

"Oh Mr. Masters, you always make me feel special," Claire said sweetly as she gave the older shop owner a soft look of the affection one might save for a grandfather.

Charles reached the front door and locked it, and while he was there, he drew the blinds quietly so nobody would see in. As

Charles approached the front of the store, Mr. Masters nodded at him. That is when Charles reached into his pocket and removed the ring case. He opened it and slipped the ring onto his finger.

Instantly Claire began to squirm in place. Charles joined Mr. Masters and Claire recognized him from parent's nights at the school. "Mr. Masters, Mr. Johnson, what is happening to me?" she said as sweat beaded from her brow. She felt her nipples instantly grow hard and her pussy seemed to be on fire with an urgent need to be fucked.

"Claire," Mr. Masters said firmly, "tell Mr. Johnson what you need right now."

"I need to be fucked," she gasped. "Oh God, I don't talk like that. Please help me. Stop this. Oh God, my pussy is too wet. Please Mr. Masters, stop me. Please Mr. Johnson, fuck me now."

"Claire, don't fall down. Use this table," Mr. Masters said firmly and helped her to lay forward on a thin display table full of costume hats. Claire fell forward as Charles raced around behind her. He looked down at the squirming schoolteacher as her hips thrust at the table inside that conservative grey skirt.

"Hurry up, Charles. Fuck her," Mr. Masters ordered. "We don't have all day."

As fast as he could, Charles pulled up that skirt, revealing the backs of Claire's sexy thighs. He yanked it all the way up to her waistline so he could get his hands on her pantyhose top and panties.

Just then, Claire reached out and got a

grip on the belt holding up Mr. Master's pants. With a wild look in her eyes, she pulled his crotch to her and unzipped his pants.

"Wait...," he gasped, but before he could stop her, she had reached in and pulled his cock out; she was pulling it to her mouth. "I am too old for this," the old storekeeper moaned as he saw his small penis stiffen in her fingers.

"Oh God please, Mr. Masters, stop me. I am not like this," Claire whispered, but she was not able to stop her mouth from taking that 4-inch cock in her mouth and beginning to suck it like a slut.

Behind her, Charles pulled the woman's pantyhose down to mid-thigh and unzipped his pants. Mr. Masters looked at him and mouthed, "Hurry" as he pulled out his rock-hard cock. He had never fucked another woman since he got married, but looking down at Claire's hairy pussy between her white thighs, he had no way of turning back.

Charles pushed those sexy thighs apart, reached in, and parted her pussy lips to see her pink slit and that sweet wet vagina hole ready to be fucked. Taking a firm stance, he leaned in and put the head of his cock in the rim.

As soon as Claire felt that cock in her slit, she moaned, "Oh God, push it in me."

Charles buried his hard shaft up to the balls in her wet pussy and began to fuck in and out of her faster and faster.

At the same time, Mr. Masters was holding Claire's head and fucking into her mouth. He was gasping from the stress but was unable to stop pushing his hard cock into her lips so she could suck him hungrily. Suddenly he stiffed up and began to gasp. "Uh uh uh," he gasped and he came in her mouth spurt after spurt. Claire had never sucked a cock, much less had it shot sperm in her mouth, but the ring had her in its power and she felt driven to swallow his cum.

"Oh God, she is swallowing," Mr. Masters gasped and that was all it took for Charles.

He bent over and grabbed Claire around the waist and started fucking her furiously. He pounded into her wet pussy so both Claire and Charles were gasping and grunting. Charles felt his orgasm hit like a steamroller and his cock exploded inside her, filling her pussy with cum.

Claire was humping back into that hard cock when it filled her with sperm. "More fucking. Oh God, stop me! Fuck me more!" she screamed. Charles zipped up his pants and stepped back, seeing the middle school teacher writhe and beg for cock like a slut.

"Do it Charles. Use the ring. Finish her."

Charles did as he was told. He pointed the ring at Claire and said firmly "Orgasm!"

Claire gasped and grabbed her pussy with her fingers and rolled to the floor, her hips bucking and wiggling. She came so hard she almost knocked the table over. Then she gasped and slumped over in a swoon.

Master of the Ring

Charles had some concern for Mr. Masters. Claire recovered and was a changed woman. She remarked that her husband never made her cum like that. She swore secrecy and asked Charles to come see her during break at the school. But Charles knew better than to have that dangerous ring anywhere near a building full of middle school girls. And there were plenty of more women to fuck other than Claire right away.

Mr. Masters recovered but confessed that he was too old for that kind of orgy. He gladly passed ownership to Charles with the vow that he would use it only as he was taught, that he would protect the innocent and the old, and that he would pass it to a worthy heir when he became unable to put the ring into its proper use.

Charles kept the ring in its lead-lined case at all times and was careful. There were so many times when he saw a girl on the street or in a store and wanted to take it out and fuck her but he could not. He was very aware of the power of the ring, and he did not want to be shouting "orgasm" at a room full of women just to get out of a tough situation.

There were odd times when the ring came in handy. Late at night after working late, Charles stopped at a convenience store. Working behind the desk was a young woman who was probably in her mid-20s. Charles had the ring in his pocket, but as he began to think about fucking her right there in the store, a patron came in, bought something, and left. Charles had learned patience. But his good sense prevailed somewhat, but not entirely.

When the car was gone, he approached the young cashier. He had brought with him a number of costly food and car supply items. With the gas, the total came to over $200. Charles handed her his credit card and took out the Ring of Passion. Just as she opened the drawer, he put it on.

"Oh my God!" she gasped, grasping the counter as her body began to explode with a need for sex. But just as she looked at him, Charles pointed the ring at her and said that word – "Orgasm."

The cashier fell to the floor behind the counter laughing and cumming, and then she swooned. Charles restrained his thoughts of fucking her anyway; instead, he took his credit card back, all the merchandise he wanted, and all of the money in the cash drawer.

Charles drove away feeling guilty, evil, and satisfied. He knew the girl would wake up from the best orgasm of her life, report it all as an unsolved robbery, and then spend her life wishing she could meet the sexy stranger who made her cum like that.

The Ultimate Prize
Over the months after getting the Ring of Passion, Charles fucked dozens of women in

town. He called his best friend's house to drop by and pick up a golf club when he knew he was not there. When his sexy wife Colleen let him in, Charles found a way to be alone in a quiet room with her. The Ring of Passion turned Colleen into a sexual animal, and Charles fucked her for two hours, leaving cum in her pussy, in her mouth, and even up her ass.

Finally, after learning to use the ring well, he set after the ultimate prize. Since that night when Charles thought pretending to be Gandalf was the ultimate in sex ploys, Elaine had been a cold fish. Charles did not worry about it too much because with the Ring of Passion, he could fuck any woman he could get in a room. But that sting of rejection stuck with him. And deep down inside, Elaine was always the sexual prize he wanted the most. Now he had his chance.

Mr. Masters was glad to see Charles return and hear all of his adventures using the ring. "I have slept much better with it gone, but I am glad you are carrying on the legacy of the ring," he said to Charles. But when Charles rented the Gandalf costume one more time, Mr. Masters was surprised. "Seducing your wife again tonight, Charles?" he said with a laugh.

"I am going for the ultimate prize tonight, Mr. Masters," Charles said with a wry smile. "But this time Gandalf really will have a ring of power and a ring of passion when he wants Elaine in every possible way."

"Oh yes. Elaine," Mr. Masters said with a knowing smile as he rented Charles the costume.

Charles did not let on to Elaine of his plans as they had their dinner. She was friendly, but not affectionate, and that had been her condition since that night. It was common for Elaine to go to bed and for Charles to stay up and watch TV. So after she was in the bedroom, Charles got out the costume and slipped it on. Under the white robes, he was nude with one other item. The ring was in its case in the pocket of the robe.

The door to the bedroom literally burst open, and there stood Charles in full Gandalf costume including a staff that he added this time. Elaine was lying on the bed looking at her smart phone when she turned over to see what this was all about. She had on a pair of shortie pajamas that showed off her sexy legs nicely.

"Don't start with this shit, Charles," Elaine said. "I had enough of this last time."

She talked tough on the outside, but she could see from the tent in those robes that he already had a huge hard-on for her. It was impossible for Elaine to forget how hot it was when he just "took" her before she threw him out for playing with her asshole.

"You will submit to me, wench," Charles said with a commanding voice, stepping to the middle of the room. He peeled open his robe and his naked body was revealed. "And you will yield to the power of the ring."

Just then, Charles held toward her his clenched fist. But that ring on his index finger was not his class ring from school. It was silver and it emitted a glow and a radiation that got to Elaine. She felt it first in her nipples, which began to buzz and get hard. Then it spread down her body to her clit and into her pussy, making it wet and feel as if it was on fire.

"Oh my God, Charles!" she gasped as her body lit up with passion and any other thought disappeared. "What is happening to me?" she gasped as her mind tried to fight the tidal wave of lust that was taking over every muscle in her body. "I can't think of anything else other than how much I want you to fuck me," she gasped as her mind objected with all it had to this undignified language.

Charles walked on his knees to the middle of the bed and saw the confusion, panic, and raw lust in the eyes of his wife. "Worship my cock, Elaine," he said in a low voice, and he put his hand on her head and pushed it down toward his rock-hard cock. Elaine wanted to fight being forced to suck her husband's penis, but she was so on fire with lust that she wanted nothing more. She fell on that hard cock and took it into her mouth, forcing more and more of it deeper and deeper until it filled her mouth and throat.

Charles walked on his knees, pushing her back until she was lying on her back with his cock in her mouth. Then he leaned on his hands, looking down at her sweet mouth full of cock, and began to fuck in and out of her mouth. Elaine's eyes were wide with shock, lust, and fear as her husband thrust his erection into her mouth, but at the same time, her pussy was aching to be fucked.

Finally, Charles pulled his cock out of her mouth and rolled her on her back. He grabbed her hair and pulled her head back, kissing her mouth hard. "I am going to fuck you in every way there is to fuck you," he growled at his wife.

Then with a power he never felt before, he grabbed her pajama top from behind and literally ripped it apart. The fabric flew everywhere. He was filled with lust and wanted her body. He yanked her panties and PJ shorts down to her knees and mounted her, biting her back and neck.

"Oh God yes," Elaine moaned from her driving inner need. "Fuck me hard," she hissed like the nympho slut that she wanted to be for her husband.

Without thinking, she arched her ass up to him and buried her face in the pillow. Charles mounted her like an animal and pushed her legs open to spread her pussy lips wide. In one sudden thrust, he buried the shaft of his cock in his wife and fucked her furiously.

Elaine had her hand down her front stroking her clit. The violation of her cunt from her husband's rock-hard shaft was the only satisfaction she could get. But before he shot his full cum, he rose and parted her butt cheeks. Elaine knew what her husband was going to do, and deep in her mind, she was horrified. But the out-of-control slut pushed her butt up to him to be fucked.

Charles looked at the tiny ass opening of her wife as he held her cheeks open. "Please

Charles, no," Elaine whispered and that turned into a deep groan of need. "Fuck me in my butt, Charles. Take it." The on-fire slut was being driven mad by the ring of passion. Charles fit the tip of his cock in that rim and began to push.

Elaine clawed at the bed at the pain of her butt opening spreading. With pressure, Charles felt the head of his cock enter his wife. She was moaning and muttering almost as if she was speaking in tongues. Deeper and deeper into her rectum, Charles drove his stiff cock. He was so close after fucking her pussy and her mouth. When his cock was halfway buried in Elaine's very tight asshole, Charles fucked in and out of it. Her moans of passion and pain as she pushed back to take his cock in that forbidden place drove him over the edge. He pushed as far as he could inside her and shot a huge load in that hole.

But finishing inside his wife did not slow her down. She fell flat on the bed with her fingers on her aroused clit, moaning and begging to be fucked more. He had to recover before pulling her into bed to fuck her all night. Charles pointed that ring at Elaine to give her relief. "ORGASM," he said and the ring did its job. She came in waves, gasping and doubling over as her pussy had the biggest orgasm of her life. Then she slept and Charles smiled with happiness that the Ring of Passion had given him the ultimate victory. His sex life with his wife would forever be passionate, out of control, and full of life and fun.

8 THE WEDDING DAY

Controlled Chaos

Oliver and Lacy had been in love since middle school. Their wedding was a cause for joy and great celebration. But as all weddings are, there was plenty of tension in the air, especially the day of the wedding. Oliver marshalled his most reliable friends, Gary and Steven, for groomsmen and to help take care of the many details that were in danger of falling through the cracks.

Oliver was willing to do this because his soon-to-be wife was by far the most beautiful girl he had ever met. She was like a princess with her wispy light blond hair that hugged her perfect pear-shaped face. She was a delicate creature with a slender and dainty figure that made Oliver crazy with passion. The thought of a night of unrestrained love making on their honeymoon drove Oliver to work hard to make this wedding perfect.

He really did like her family, including her mom and dad and her two younger sisters, Jamie who was 22 and Cindy who was 19. Both of them had that same amazingly princess-like beauty, but they were no match for his future wife in Oliver's mind. Little did he know that ever since they started dating, both of Lacy's sisters had huge crushes on him.

Wedding week was a case of controlled chaos. Everybody in both families was on the go to make it the wedding of the century. Lacy's dad had secured a huge estate for all of the wedding events, and the house was elegant from the front door to the kitchen. By the time Friday night came and the rehearsal dinner was ready to be served, the nervousness was somewhat down even though a great deal had to be done the next day. But Oliver wanted to enjoy the dinner and all of the toasts that would go with it.

After the rehearsal in the big hall, the very large wedding party adjourned to a reception room where there was a bar and plenty of room for everyone to just relax and talk as they waited for the dinner to be served. Oliver looked across the room at his bride Lacy. She looked so happy and beautiful. This was her weekend and that smile on her face meant everything to him.

The drinks flowed freely from the open bar and Oliver felt pretty good. Nature made its call and Oliver slipped out to find a bathroom. He also enjoyed wandering around the huge mansion and looking in the many big rooms. It was nice to be away from the group to catch his thoughts. So after he finished in the elegant bathroom, he explored.

Just then, as he came out of what looked like a study or a den, he saw Lacy's sister Cindy coming out of the bathroom that was designated for girls. She smiled at him, gave him a cheerful "Hi Oliver," and moved toward the stairs to go down to the party. She was wearing a very cute green dress that was cut about mid-thigh and showed off her figure nicely. She was somewhat shorter than either of her sisters, but that added to how cute she was.

Oliver was concerned because the 19-year-old looked a little unstable. She had a few drinks like everyone else so her walk was a little wobbly. He stepped forward and saw that she was about to stumble, which at the top of the stairs could have been a disaster. He gripped her by the back of the arm and pulled her to him. That is when Cindy's legs gave out and Oliver scooped her up and carried her into that den to recover.

He thought this might look bad, so he closed the door and sat with her so she did not topple off of the couch. Cindy sat up and looked at Oliver with what could only be called bedroom eyes.

"You saved me," she said with a throaty whisper.

"No, no," Oliver objected. "Just helping out. You are almost my sister-in-law, after all," he said with his hand on the soft skin of her back for support.

"No, you saved me," she insisted. "That means I belong to you."

The young girl continued letting the drinks she had enjoyed be part of the discussion. Cindy leaned into Oliver, and without warning, she kissed him full on the mouth. Oliver grunted and resisted putting his hands on her soft shoulders, but her tiny tongue entered his mouth and something in him sucked it and kissed her back.

Cindy started breathing hard, making out with her future brother-in-law, and she slid the dress down over her arms so that her gorgeous breasts popped out of the top. As Oliver pushed his tongue into her mouth, Cindy took his hands and guided them to her naked tits. Suddenly, Oliver was feeling the soft skin of her naked breasts and fondling them, one in each hand. The shock of what was happening hit Oliver suddenly and he pulled back, looking at the sexy view of those perfectly round tits that Cindy was giving him.

This was so wrong to be playing with the naked tits of his future wife's sexy younger sister. But those tits were impossible to resist as he pushed her back onto the couch and leaned in to kiss and suck them. Cindy wrapped her skinny arms around his head and moaned happily, feeling her left nipple in his mouth as he sucked it.

Oliver sat up on his knees on the couch. "We can't do this Cindy. It's so wrong," he said, but his hands were going at lightning speed pulling his shirt out of his pants and unzipping his fly.

"I know, Oliver," Cindy gasped as she pulled up her skirt and wigged her pantyhose down to her knees. "I love my sister so much," she whimpered, opening her legs to show him a glorious view of her pussy. Oliver pushed his pants down just enough to release his large, rock hard cock pointing straight at Cindy's open cunt.

"This is immoral and we could ruin our lives," he said in a low voice with his eyes staring at the lips of Cindy's pussy as she parted them to reveal her very wet vagina ready for his big cock. His words were right, but the passions were out of control. He fell onto her kissing and sucking her neck.

"Oh I know," Cindy moaned, kissing his ear. "Fuck me so we can go back," she whispered.

Her future brother-in-law's hard cock pressed against her vagina rim pushing it open to let him inside her body. Then in a moment, the head pushed inside and Oliver felt his shaft pushing deeper and deeper into the young woman. He began to fuck her slowly but with increasing speed. Oliver reached around and gripped the slender ass cheeks of his sexy sister-in-law to be, and fucked her harder and harder.

"Oh yes, Oliver! Fuck me deep," she moaned and that was all it took. Oliver grunted and buried his full shaft in her and shot a massive load of cum inside her warm, wet pussy chamber.

Morning Jitters

When Oliver and Cindy returned to the party, nobody was the least bit suspicious. Oliver had her return first and then he came back in, and when he rejoined his friends, he made eye contact with his beloved Lacy and she blew him a kiss. She would not have been so loving if she had known that the groom who would make his vows to her tomorrow had just fucked her sister.

Otherwise, the rehearsal dinner went off perfectly. Each time Oliver caught the eye of Cindy, she giggled and blushed, but she did that a lot anyway. He had always had a friendly and slightly flirty relationship with Cindy and Jamie, so a little bit of blushing was considered healthy, and it made Lacy happy to see how great her sisters thought her new husband was.

Oliver did not sleep with Lacy that night and in fact, they had only had sex a few times. Lacy had been raised in the church so she had scruples about premarital sex. That didn't hold them back, and he had been inside her pussy three times. Many more times they would be making out in the car, and she would unzip his pants, slide his cock out, and stroke him up and down until he shot his load on her hand and dress.

The morning of the wedding was a busy one. Oliver and Lacy's dad made it a point to stay handy at the mansion to set up chairs, meet vendors making deliveries, or calm nervous bridesmaids or the mother of the bride. At 10 a.m., the massage service showed up with a small army to deliver massages. Lacy's mother knew she was going to need one, so she ordered them for every female in the wedding party. Oliver had a list so he directed the men and women in white uniforms to the various rooms around the mansion to give the massages.

That all seemed to be going nicely. Oliver patrolled the halls just to kill the time. He thought about how if felt to have his cock inside of Cindy. He had to make himself stop because he kept getting a hard on. Suddenly, the door to one of the rooms opened and a woman in a white uniform rushed out. She ran up to him recognizing that he was in charge of the massages for all the women.

"Mr. Oliver, I am so sorry," she said emotionally. "My son was hurt at a ball game. I have to go." And she ran down the stairs and out the front door.

Oliver was at a loss so he walked through the door to see who was not getting a massage. There on the table laid the beautiful body of his other future sister-in-law, Jamie. She was naked, but her butt and much of her thighs were covered with a large towel. Quickly Oliver turned around and looked the other way so as not to embarrass her.

"Savannah, I liked the vanilla oil to rub my back," Jamie said looking away. Oliver was more than nervous.

"Jamie," he finally said as softly as he could. He heard the ruffle of the sheets. "Jamie, be calm. Savannah had to go because her son was hurt at a ball game. I backed in so I didn't see anything."

"Oh my god, Oliver!" Jamie said, sitting up holding the sheet to her shoulders. "Ok, let me catch my breath. You gave me quite a start."

"I know Jamie. I just felt I needed to tell you she left and why. I don't know if I have another worker to give you your massage. I will go look," he said, reaching for the door.

"No, wait Oliver!" Jamie said with a soft calm in her voice. He paused still looking away. Jamie giggled. "Oliver you can turn around, I am covered with a sheet."

He turned around and smiled nervously. Jamie was just as beautiful as her two sisters. Both Cindy and Lacy had gorgeous blond hair although Cindy's was softer brown blond and Lacy's was a soft almost white blond shade. But Jamie had a gorgeous head of striking red hair that flowed down over her the curves of her sexy shoulders.

It was impossible for Oliver not to stare at those shoulders. Jamie smiled seeing his eyes on her skin, and she liked that she could still hold the stare of a gorgeous guy like her future brother-in-law. Finally, she broke the tension.

"Listen. A massage is not rocket science. I mainly wanted some kinks taken out of my shoulders and back and some lotion put on me. You have strong hands so you will probably do the job even better than Savannah. Do you mind?" she asked with a coy sound to her voice.

At that, Jamie skilfully swivelled on the bed and laid on her front without revealing anything compromising to Oliver. She let the sheet fall below her waist, but her ample breasts were pressed into the bed. All Oliver could see was the soft skin of her shoulders and back and her legs and lower thighs. But that was a very tempting sight.

Oliver stood over the slender body of his future sister-in-law and just put his fingers on her shoulders. But as soon as he started to squeeze and massage, the feeling of her soft skin and the muscles responding underneath began to get to him. How did professionals keep from having hard-ons all the time, he wondered. He worked down onto the soft back of the sexy girl, massaging her, which was a cheap disguise for feeling her up.

"Oh that is nice, Oliver. You have strong hands," Jamie said in a low sexy voice. Then she looked up at him, leancd back on one elbow, smiled, and made a joke. "You could do this for a living."

Oliver was not sure if Jamie meant to or not, but doing that gave him a beautiful view of her right breast hanging from her body like sweet fruit ready to be eaten. Oliver's face turned bright red, but he could not take his eyes off of that round pink nipple on display for him. Her tits were bigger than her sister's and the nipples rounder as well.

When Jamie saw where his eyes were, at first she was embarrassed. Then she saw the big bulge in his pants and that made her excited. Here was the man who would be marrying her sister in a few hours, and he had a massive hard-on for her. Jamie felt she needed to remove the tension from the situation so she said, "It's ok Oliver. You can look at my tit. We are almost related, you know."

That did not make that hard-on go down. But then, Jamie was very interested in that hard-on. She reached out, took Oliver's closest hand, put it on her breast, and let him softly squeeze it. Oliver leaned forward with his other hand on the table, stared at her chest, and stroked her nipple with his fingers.

"Mmmm that is good Oliver," she cooed and she rolled over so the other tit was available to him. "Do you like my tits, Oliver?" she asked seductively.

"Oh God, Jamie! This is not right. I am marrying Lacy tonight," he moaned, but he could not resist beginning to feel her other breast. His face was getting closer and closer to suck her nipples.

"Are my tits as sexy as my sister's?" Jamie asked. That was so out of line that Oliver almost panicked thinking about the younger sister Cindy and when he fucked her the night before. As outrageous as that was for Jamie to say that, it made Oliver even more turned on for his middle sister-in-law to be.

"Oh god, Jamie! You are so sexy. I want to

fuck you," Oliver said knowing how very wrong that was. Jamie lost any control she had, and she pushed the sheet off so her naked hips and pussy were open to Oliver. She reached down, unzipped his pants, slipped in, and found the hard cock that was waiting there for her. She held it in her hand, stroking it up and down, pulling Oliver onto the table with her.

Oliver could not believe he was going to fuck the last sister of the three in the family, and before his wedding to boot. He wiggled his pants down and moved over Jamie's leg so she could spread her sexy thighs wide to let him get into her pussy. Jamie looked up at this man who was about to be family and gasped at how hot and muscular he was. His big cock stuck out from the public hair, and she could see the testicles that would be putting cum in her any minute.

Suddenly, she saw the clock above the door. "Oliver, in a half hour the time for massages are over. Fuck me!" she said obscenely and she pulled him down on to her.

Oliver fell onto Jamie and began to kiss her neck and lick her shoulders. Jamie moved her hand under her thigh, found Oliver's hard cock, and moved it to the opening of her cunt. As soon as Oliver felt the warmth and wet of the rim of her vagina, he pushed and slid inside her easily.

Both Oliver and Jamie gasped when he fully penetrated her. He began to fuck in and out of her powerfully with a lust that was driven by the time and how wrong this all was. He even lifted up and looked into the eyes of his future wife's sister. She had no resistance when he kissed her mouth and slid his tongue inside her lips.

"Oh god Oliver, harder!" Jamie gasped, pulling him down to her tits where he began to kiss and suck them. His cock slammed in and out of her faster and faster.

"I am going to cum," he moaned, pushing up to pull out of Jamie, but she thrust up with her hips and impaled herself on his big hard cock. That was all he could take and he shot a huge load in Jamie, filling the deep place of her pussy with streams of hot sperm from his balls.

Here Comes the Bride

Oliver had no sooner filled Jamie with cum when they heard footsteps in the hallway. He hopped off of her, pulled up his pants, and escaped by another room just as the massage service came in. He heard Jamie explain what happened and accepted their apologies and then she dismissed them. Oliver had the urge to run in there and fuck her again but he knew better, so he dashed down the stairs to find out where all of the big goals of the day were and what he could do to pull off this big wedding.

The rest of the morning was quieter because the women in the wedding party were in another part of the property getting their hair, makeup, and nails done. Oliver had a chance to get away and have a walk around the grounds to catch his breath. But he could not be gone for long. As he approached the mansion, he saw his beautiful bride Lacy on the terrace looking sad. But when he approached, she brightened up.

"I have missed you so much," she said, holding him close and kissing him. Oliver breathed a silent sigh of relief because he briefly worried she knew that he had fucked both of her sisters in the last 24 hours. "I know it is bad luck to see each other, but I will be calmer with your kisses," she whispered. They kissed for a few moments and then Lacy started to pull away.

"Lots more where that came from tonight lover," she teased him. Then she whispered in his ear. "I am going to fuck your brains out tonight, husband." And she moved toward the terrace doors. "Oh honey, Mom is down in the chapel and she is freaking out. Could you see if she needs any help?"

When Oliver entered the chapel, Mrs. Worthington was scurrying around the room straightening chairs and fussing with the flowers. She was in a panic about all the arrangements. "Linda," Oliver addressed her and she jumped with a start. Oliver agreed to call Lacy's parents by their first names until the wedding and then after that to address them as mom and dad.

"Oh, Oliver, I am so glad you are here. Would you get those candle holders down?"

Oliver got on a chair and got the four candleholders down, and he helped his future mother-in-law arrange them with fake leaves and some gorgeous pillar candles she had for the occasion. She had on the dress she had picked out for the wedding and the reception. It was probably a $1000 dress at least, and it accented her shapely legs and hips beautifully. The neck came down to reveal just enough cleavage, but not too much.

As Lacy's mom was fussing with the candles, she bent over and Oliver got a great view down her top. She had shapely breasts and her bra was the same dark purple shade as the dress. But Oliver's eyes were sharp and he caught a peek out of that bra of her left nipple. He was so angry with himself.

Just then, Linda looked up and saw her future son-in-law catching a peek down her top. She smiled broadly at him. "I think someone is very ready for the honeymoon night," she teased him. She got a chuckle when the sweet boy blushed. In her mind, he was just a kid who had not been laid for days, if not weeks. Little did she know where that cock had been. "It's alright Oliver," she said softly. "I understand you are so ready for sex with my daughter. You are allowed. You are making an honest woman of her."

Oliver knew Lacy's mom to be a bit of a wild card, but this all came after he had his cock inside of two of her three daughters so he felt a bit dizzy from it all. "Tell you what we will do. I will help to tide you over." At that, Oliver's future mother-in-law unzipped his pants right in the middle of the chapel where he would be married in a matter of hours.

She knelt down in front of him, reached in, and found that his cock was already hard as a rock. "Oh this is nice. Let me get a sneak peek at the big old cock that my daughter will enjoy tonight."

Linda looked up to see Oliver gazing with lust at her tits. She was flattered and excited to be looked at like that again after so many boring years of marriage. She couldn't resist so she released two buttons of that elegant dress so it opened in front. Then she reached in and released the clasp on her bra so it pulled away.

Oliver hardly knew what to do as he stared at Linda's gorgeous tits swaying back and forth while she knelt in front of him. He was even more blown away when his future mother-in-law pulled that hard cock to her lips and licked it. That was just a little test because in moments her mouth opened wide and she took his entire cock into her mouth up to the balls.

"Oh god!" Oliver gasped, feeling his full erection being expertly sucked by this amazingly sexy woman. Oliver held her head and moved his cock in and out of her mouth but he had trouble keeping his footing. Just then, he stumbled and stepped back a few feet from the horny mother of the bride. There was a sound a little ways up the hall. It was only a worker putting up supplies but it alarmed Linda so she stood up.

"This is dangerous Oliver and sinful to do this with each other just before you marry

Lacy." She turned from him, walked toward the front of the chapel, and faced the low podium where the bible would be. Just as she was about to fasten her bra back, she felt Oliver behind her. By this time, any sense of right and wrong had vanished from Oliver. He slipped his arms around her middle and then grasped each one of those sexy tits and held them while he began to kiss and suck her neck.

"Oh god, Oliver! We could be caught. This is wrong..." Linda whispered, but she leaned over and put her hands on that alter and pushed her butt up to him. This was becoming a drill for Oliver because he knew that the chapel was open and people would be moving this way within an hour. He was shocked that his cock was so hard for Lacy's mom, but his lust was boiling in his blood.

"I know, Linda. Oh god we have to stop!" he said in a low voice but instead of stopping, Oliver put his hands on the hem of that elegant skirt and pulled it up her thighs until it was over her hips. Then he worked her pantyhose down until her naked ass was revealed to him. Rudely, he thrust his fingers between her round white thighs and found the moist and soft folds of her pussy. Instantly, Lacy's mom responded by moaning and spreading her thighs open and bending further to push her pussy toward that long hard cock she had been sucking.

"Fuck me, Oliver!" she said with an out of control sound to her voice. Oliver was way ahead of her leaning in and moving the tip of his cock to the opening of this woman who was the mother of his bride. In a swift thrust, he filled Linda's vagina, spreading it open with his large cock. Linda gasped feeling him penetrate her and held on to the altar.

Oliver leaned into the sexy woman and wrapped his arms around her. He started fucking in and out of her furiously, feeling the warmth of her cunt suck him deep into her hole. "Yes, yes, yes!" he heard Linda moan as she pushed back and up so he could get all of his cock inside her with each thrust. Suddenly, he felt Linda begin to shudder and her pussy constricted around him. She made gurgling noises and she had an orgasm right there in the middle of the chapel.

That was all Oliver could stand. He came in her with his cock buried full shaft in her sexy pussy.

Oliver and Linda had just enough time to put themselves together when a few people drifted in to check on the arrangements. Two hours later Oliver stood at that altar and took Lacy to be his wife. As he said those words of commitment, it was impossible not to think about the fact that he had fucked every woman in this family and would be fucking Lacy at their honeymoon suite tonight. But it was when he said the final promise with those words, "I do" that all around that chapel, his mother-in-law and two sisters-in-law, thought to themselves, "Oh yes! You do, Oliver, and you will do again."

9 THE INNER MAGIC

Preface

Emma was not a beautiful girl. As much as family and friends talked about her inner beauty, the mirror does not lie. It was particularly obvious living with a gorgeous girl like Amanda. Amanda had that classic beauty of perfect skin, the face of an angel, fluffy blond hair, and a slender sexy body with perky tits to catch the eye of any boy. In almost every way, Emma was the opposite of her roommate. Her skin was damaged from acne in her teens. The shape of her face was odd and her hair was drab. While she was not fat, her body was shapeless and the only way boys looked at her was to look away.

Like most girls who have to come to terms with not being the beauty queen, Emma found other ways to get self-worth. She took a lot of comfort that Amanda liked her just as she was. It was not a sympathy friendship and Amanda was happy to be seen in public with her when they went out to shop or eat. Amanda also worked with Emma to get her hairstyle shaped up and to find a wardrobe that helped. But Emma often observed that you can put lipstick on a pig but it is still a pig.

Amanda and Emma met for lunch at their favorite Chinese restaurant. They always had the best time eating there as they gossiped and made jokes like best friends do. But at the end of the meal, a surprise came in the fortune cookie. Emma opened hers and read it silently. Then she said, "This is the weirdest fortune I have ever read."

Emma handed the fortune to Amanda who read it out loud. "A golden drop of life will change you forever. With that drop, the beauty that is on your insides will be on your outsides." Both girls looked at each other. Finally, they giggled and forgot all about it, except Emma kept that fortune in her purse.

When Watching Has to Do

While Emma felt accepted and liked when she was with her family or with Amanda, there was no getting around it that it was easy for Amanda to have a love life as sexy as she was. Emma gave up trying to lose her virginity because boys just were not interested. One way Emma learned to have an exciting sexual life was to live it through Amanda by watching her fuck her boyfriends when they came over.

At first, Emma had to find ways to peek. Finally, she had to confess to her best friend what she was doing. Emma was shocked when Amanda fell backward on the couch giggling and holding her hand. "I thought I saw you girl!" she squealed. "Were you masturbating while you watched us?" Amanda asked with a laugh.

"Yes I was," Emma answered shyly. "So you are not mad?"

"The opposite, girl!" Amanda laughed. "Between you and I, it gets me kinda exciting knowing you are watching."

So the girls hatched a plan to make it easier for Emma to watch. They created a "window" in the wall of the closet between the two bedrooms of the apartment. Then, Amanda agreed to position herself with her boyfriend on the bed so Emma could see well and to leave the clothes in the closet parted so Emma could see through.

The first chance to try out the window came the next Friday when Amanda had her boyfriend, Jackson, over. She told him that Emma was not home when, in fact, she was waiting quietly in her room. Amanda and Jackson started making out on the couch and she knew he was turned on when he pulled down her top and began feeling her naked breasts while sucking her neck.

"I want to fuck you, babe," he moaned.

"Me too, sexy," Amanda whispered back.

"But let's go to my room in case Emma comes home."

The plan was working like a charm. Emma had her lights off so no light could come through the window in the closet wall. Amanda brought Jackson into her bedroom and she kissed him and guided him to sit on the bed facing the closet. Jackson kissed his girlfriend, brought his hand up, and started feeling her left tit. Emma watched those fingers close over that perfect breast and then she saw him pull down her top revealing the round naked tit of her best friend.

Emma began to get turned on so she very quietly slipped her shorts and panties down so she could masturbate. She felt her own fingers on her clit as Jackson leaned down and pulled Amanda's top and bra off and then leaned down and began to kiss and suck her nipples. Amanda moaned with pleasure and looked over at the dark closet where she knew Emma's eyes were watching silently.

Smiling in the direction of Emma, Amanda slipped her hand to the pants of her boyfriend and unzipped his fly. The boy was moaning and sucking her eagerly going from one perfect tit to the other one. But he felt her slender fingers slip into his pants, slide skillfully into his shorts, and grasp his already very hard cock; he leaned back to let her pleasure him.

Emma could see it all perfectly and knowing that her best friend deliberately was revealing her boyfriend's hard cock to her with their little scheme made it all even more exciting. Amanda pulled out that stiff penis and stroked it up and down. Emma looked at Jackson's amazing cock and stroked her clit gently trying to sustain the tremendous pleasure she was experiencing. That was when Amanda suddenly smiled toward where Emma's hiding place was in the closet and lowered her lips to suck Jackson's cock lustfully.

"Oh yes babe, suck it," Jackson moaned, feeling his gorgeous girlfriend take the head in her warm and wet mouth and begin to suck. Emma stroked her clit and slipped a finger to her wet pussy hole and played with the rim trying not to moan watching Amanda take Jackson's full cock in her mouth, slide it out all wet and then lower her mouth over it again, pumping it in and out of her lips.

Jackson laid back on the bed, moaning and pushing his hard cock up into his girlfriend's mouth faster and faster. "Oh god baby, I am going to cum!" he gasped. Just then, Amanda took it out of her mouth and moved her hand up and down that wet cock looking at the closet where her best friend was watching. Like a volcano going off, Jackson's orgasm shot streams of white cum high into the air over his cock. The thick cum goo landed in her hair and covered her face. The boy's body bucked and orgasmed over and over, getting cum all over his own crotch and on Amanda as well.

Within moments, Jackson was groggy and he rolled over on Amanda's bed and dozed off. Amanda dashed out of her room and into Emma's. As she opened the door, she saw that Emma was on the bed with her panties pushed down. Emma reached her orgasm from what she just saw as Amanda entered and Amanda watched the amazing sight of Emma's skinny finger moving in and out of her tight hole as she came.

Amanda ran to the bed and leaped onto it giggling like a child. "Emma did you see?" She giggled.

Emma looked up at her beautiful friend and said in a low whisper. "That was so hot!" Then, she smiled at how much cum was still all over Amanda's face, hair, and neck. Just then, a tiny ball of cum formed up on the top of Amanda's eyebrow. It shaped itself into a perfect sphere and began to detach from that tiny spot.

Emma was hypnotized by that tiny droplet of cum. Slowly, it released itself and launched into the air. The dim light from her lamp shimmered off of the surface of the cum drop as it fell toward her face. It seemed to shimmer with magic and emit a golden glow. Just then, the words of that fortune echoed in her mind.

"A golden drop of life will change you forever. With that drop, the beauty that is on your insides will be on your outsides."

That golden drop of life fell faster and faster toward Emma's face. Something in her responded to it and she opened her mouth. That tiny bit of cum from Jackson's cock fell into Emma's mouth and rested on her tongue. Then, as if it was a precious taste of fine wine, Emma swallowed it.

Magic

Suddenly, a bright flash burst inside the room. It was so sudden that both girls were blinded for several minutes. Emma heard Amanda scream and fall off of the bed onto the floor. When Emma could see again, she had trouble focusing a little bit. She saw Amanda stand up on the other side of the bedroom. Emma was still lying on the bed, but it was no longer the same bed. Everything had changed.

The room was no longer a regular American apartment bedroom. It was more rustic like it was in a hut or a cabin. The bed was not the same either. It was like a bed of straw and the blanket was a handmade quilt. Even the clothing that both girls were wearing was different. They had on what seemed like peasant girls costumes from the Middle Ages. Amanda looked up and down at herself and she shrieked. "Oh my god Emma!"

"What is it Amanda?" Emma said in a panic.

"You!" Amanda answered. "Look at yourself." There was a handheld mirror sitting on a basket in the corner. None of this stuff was in that room seconds before. Amanda rushed over and took the mirror to Emma. Emma gasped at what she saw in that mirror.

She was stunningly beautiful. Instead of the plain and homely girl that she used to see in the mirror, a ravenous beauty looked back. She had jet-black hair that flowed over her shoulders like a waterfall. Her face was like a model's with high cheekbones and perfect skin. Her lips were full and sexy and her shoulders and chest that were showing in the simple dress she had on were perfectly contoured.

"Amanda, I just thought what happened," Emma said gasping as she jumped to her feet. "Remember that weird fortune?" she said.

"Yes it was so weird. It was like 'A golden drop of life will change you forever. With that drop, the beauty that is on your insides will be on your outsides'," she remembered. "But I don't get it."

"It happened, Amanda," Emma said with excitement. "One drop of cum that was on your face fell in my mouth. It was a golden drop of life and now look at me!" Just then, the girls heard sounds like men on horseback outside the door. This made no more sense than anything else did, because the apartment was on the second floor. But that reality had disappeared.

The Princess and the Knight of the Round Table

Both girls dashed out of the bedroom door, and they found themselves outside a rustic Middle Ages house. They were in peasant girl outfits, barefoot. Rapidly approaching were three mounted riders. The one in the lead wore colorful clothing like royalty. The other two were in uniforms. All three of them rode without a helmet and they were so gorgeous that in modern times, they would be supermodels. The three horses approached the slender peasant girls and stopped.

"Greetings. I am Sir Lancelot. These are my aids Phillip and Sean." The other handsome riders nodded. "We must rest our horses," Lancelot said and then his eyes made contact with Emma's. The Knight of the Round Table was stunned by Emma's overpowering beauty. He dismounted and approached her. "How is it a princess like you is in this peasant setting?" With that, he swooped her up in his arms.

Emma gasped and squealed at how handsome and strong he was. She ran her slender fingers through his long blond hair. As though it was commissioned by the gods, Lancelot kissed Emma deeply and began to walk toward the peasant hut that the girls had come out of.

"That leaves this stunning beauty for us," Phillip said as both of the aides dismounted and approached Amanda. Amanda giggled with excitement as the handsome riders looked at her with nothing else but pure lust. Sean picked her up and buried his face in her neck kissing and sucking it as Phillip created an opening in big field of very tall wheat so they could take her there to ravish her.

Lancelot took his princess into the hut and laid her on the bed kissing her mouth passionately. He knelt on the bed and peeled off the flowery shirt revealing his muscular chest with no hair on it at all. All Emma could do was softly whisper "Oh" as he leaned over kissing her on her lips and down her neck to her shoulders. She let her fingers trace the hard muscles of Lancelot's shoulders and arms.

Emma was in heaven, being made love to by a sexy and handsome knight. She opened her blouse and let it fall back revealing her perfectly round breasts. The spell that made her gorgeous had also made her very sexy. "Oh my princess," the sexy knight moaned as he leaned in and kissed her nipples and began to lick them while his strong hands squeezed her tits and pushed them together.

Emma arched her back to push her ample new tits up to the excited prince to suck and bite. At the same time, he was pulling up her peasants skirt and letting his hands roam all over the cool soft skin of her knees and then her thighs. This would be Emma's first time so she gave into anything this amazing Knight of the Round Table wanted to take from her.

Lancelot leaned over her, parting her slender thighs with his muscular legs. He kissed her mouth hard pushing his tongue into her lips for her to taste. Emma explored the outer muscles of his rock-hard legs with her slender fingers. She felt the soft hair of those thighs and then followed his flesh to his well-toned ass cheeks.

The sexy knight slid Emma's panties off and then thrust his fingers into her slit to prepare her body to be penetrated. "Oh yes," Emma moaned feeling the delicate folds of her pussy opened to his probing fingers. "Take me," she whispered to him and she lifted her hips to offer him the entrance to her womb.

When Emma felt that strong and very hard cock begin to spread open her vagina rim, she moaned and gasped at the feeling of being entered. The head of Lancelot's big cock stretched her opening and pushed inside her. Emma felt the pain of her virginity giving in as that big cock pushed deeper and deeper. But with it broken, he plunged the full shaft in her.

He was commanding and urgent as he fucked his new princess deep inside her cunt, on her own straw bed. At the same time, he kissed her tenderly and stroked her hair with each powerful thrust inside her vagina. Soon, he began to speed up and the pain began to disappear. Emma thrust up to fuck Lancelot back meeting his thrusts one by one. As her clit rubbed into his huge hips, she was overwhelmed with passion and she cried out so loud it was heard outside as she had her orgasm.

Emma's orgasm set off the handsome knight who buried his hard cock deep in her and shot massive loads of cum to fill her womanhood with his seed.

The Ravishing of Amanda

Out in the tall wheat, Phillip and Sean poured their desire into making love to Amanda. The wheat lay down like a soft bed as Sean kissed Amanda's mouth and began to feel her soft tits through her peasant's gown. It was hard to focus entirely on the hot kisses Sean was giving her because at her feet, Phillip was pulling off the gear he wore to protect the prince.

Each piece that fell off revealed more of his sexy body. Soon she looked at his sexy chest and watched him slide his tights down. Instantly what sprang out from his body was his long and very hard cock ready to ravish the maiden in the soft wheat. Sean pulled free from those deep kisses to take off his uniform and Phillip took over. He fell forward into Amanda's legs pushing up her skirt and kissing her naked legs as the sunlight showed her sexy thighs.

Amanda watched Sean strip while becoming more and more lustful watching his friend lick his way up to her sweet pussy. As he began to lick up and down her wet slit and pleasure the maiden's clit, Sean was on Amanda kissing her aggressively and pulling her top open to play with her tits. With one pair of strong hands holding her thighs far apart so he could pleasure her and another making her soft tits his toys, Amanda felt like she was being ravished by experts and she was loving it.

Amanda was on fire to be fucked hard by either or both of these amazing warriors. She did not have to wait long. Phillip crawled forward and thrust his hips into her pussy valley, holding his hard cock to help it find her wet insides. Meanwhile, Amanda was thrusting her tongue into Sean's mouth and stroking his long hard cock that was just at her arms length away. She moaned with happy passion as the big aide to Sir Lancelot filled her cunt with his big cock and began to fuck her.

To Sean's surprise, Amanda twisted under Phillip until her mouth reached that big dangling cock and she slipped the head into her mouth and started sucking him hard as she felt Phillip fucking in and out of the hole between her legs. The moaning and slapping of skin together coming out of that field of wheat was enough to start local legends. But it was the loud gasps and groans that came from three orgasms at once that really scared the locals. Amanda came hard with two big hard cocks to pleasure her and that was enough to put the two warriors over the top. Sean came in her mouth and Phillip shot his load inside of Amanda, filling her up with cum.

The Golden Drop of Life

Emma did not want to lose the wonderful feeling of her prince buried deep in her pussy, pumping it full of cum. He kissed her as they heard the moans of passion coming from the field outside where Amanda was being ravished. When it became quiet, Lancelot whispered to Emma "I will shower you with riches and make you my bride."

"I want that," Emma moaned with happiness to the man who took her virginity. She didn't care if she ever went back to her own world. Regretfully, the knight let his penis slip out of the satisfied vagina of his princess.

"I can sense that my aides have finished ravishing the maiden, too. I will prepare for our trip to the castle where you will be mine forever," he said lovingly. But before he pulled away, she pulled his big leg to her face as he stood over her. His beautiful cock dangled over her face with small globs of cum still oozing out of it.

Just then a tiny round droplet of the cum of Sir Lancelot formed at the end of his long penis. It took a perfect shape and fell from that skin toward the face of the happy princess Emma. As it fell, it took on that golden shine that Emma recognized from before. It began to spin as it dropped and without thinking, Emma opened her lips. That perfectly shaped droplet of golden cum hit her tongue and she gathered it in and swallowed it.

A Lasting Spell

Lancelot was putting his royal garments in place as his aides were putting themselves together as well. They looked down on the happily ravished maiden Amanda and vowed they would return to take her to the courtyard and make her their regular strumpet for sex every day. That sounded just fine to Amanda.

Amanda sat up to gather her garments that were thrown all over that wheat field, and then she looked up to the sky. At the same time, Emma sat up and gasped "NO." That violent flash of light hit like a bolt of lightning. Both girls were thrown down and blinded temporary and both wept because they knew what this meant.

When Emma was able to see again, she was back in her bedroom in their apartment. There were no knights or horses. Suddenly, Amanda burst through the door and she was as baffled as Emma was. They hugged and cried and then they laughed with joy at their experience. At first, they questioned if they dreamed it all. But then Emma found straw in Amanda's hair and they both had bite marks on their necks and shoulders from their royal lovers from King Arthur's court.

But then, Amanda suddenly gasped. "Emma there is one more thing that never went away from our adventure," she said with a low whisper of awe. At that, she held up the mirror. Emma looked in that mirror and staring back at her was that stunning, raven-haired princess that Sir Lancelot had loved. That part of the spell would never go away.

Amanda checked the apartment and found a note from Jackson. "Sweetie. You and Emma must have gone out. I will call you tomorrow." Amanda brought the note to Emma and both of them just stared at it because it proved that they really were gone. As the day passed into evening, the girls were happy to sit on that bed and relive an amazing experience that nobody else would understand.

They lit candles because they never wanted to stop feeling like princesses. With soft music on to keep the mood, Amanda looked at her now beautiful friend and said softly, "You really are as beautiful on the outside as on the inside Emma. I hope this spell never wears off." The two girls felt so bonded that it seemed natural what happened next.

Tears of happiness formed in Emma's eyes and Amanda dabbed them, laughing and crying at the same time for how she changed into such a gorgeous creature. That was when without thinking about it, Amanda leaned in and kissed Emma on the lips. It was as much about their bond and the caring between them than it was about kissing.

Still, that kiss led to another and another. The candles and soft music put the girls in just the right mood. Soon, Emma opened her lips and their tongues explored each other's mouths in deep and loving kisses. Emma found her body responding to the deep kisses of her best friend so she slid her hand between her legs to stroke her clit. That is when she found her pussy was a mess of dried and still moist cum oozing from her insides from the deep fucking she got from Sir Lancelot.

"Amanda," she whispered holding her to her neck. "We are full of their cum." Amanda let her own fingers slip into her panties to discover large quantities of ancient cum in her. Both girls laughed and cried about that. They wanted to preserve the cum of those lovers but good sense took over and they jumped in the big tub in the apartment they shared.

The evening passed happily, as the girls enjoyed soaping each other in a hot bubble bath, kissing, and touching each other in the warm water. Then, they took their joy to the bed and made love to each other so they could enjoy another new level of orgasms.

10 IN THE DARK

Dana loved to go to the movies alone in the middle of the day. It wasn't that she could not get dates. At 21, she had a gorgeous look that was often described as adorable. She was a petite girl with short hair that she wore to the shoulders. She had a cute figure that was not overly sensual, but it often drew the attention of males of all ages.

Dana also had a very well developed sense of style. Even if she was just going out to run errands, she dressed to look her best. Many had told her - and she believed them - that among her most sexy attributes were her very sexy legs. So she made it a point to keep them tanned and to wear short skirts to show them off, even if she was not going somewhere to flirt with boys her age.

Even if she was attending a matinee, she

dressed well, and it gave the ushers plenty of joy selling her the ticket, popcorn, and escorting her to a seat. She came to the movie theatre almost every week, not only because she enjoyed that privileged treatment, but also because the high school or college boys who worked there liked her sexy legs.

Her habit of going to the movies started after a bad break-up. Dana found that if she went to a busy and loud movie, if she did need to cry she could let it out. The excitement of the movies often made the pain go away for a while. But then, when the memory of that failed romance long vanished, Dana continued to enjoy the experience of being in the dark and letting a good movie take her into another world.

The Watcher

Dana's habit of dressing nicely when she went out was also part of the ritual of going to the movies by herself. The payoff was the attention she got from others at the movies and from the ushers and workers at the theatre. Since it was summer, the guys working there were almost always horny high school or college guys. Dana was quite interested in a couple of them, but she had a rule that the ritual of going to the movies by herself was not a tool for getting picked up. It was "me time" for Dana, dating back to when she started after that break-up.

Things began to change one Thursday afternoon. Dana had gotten settled in her seat on the second row of the balcony. This was the perfect spot because it was almost always empty, and she felt secluded to her thoughts. Most of the time, there were hardly anyone else in the theatre. But just before the lights went down, a family entered.

This no cause for alarm as it was a Disney movie about to be played. Dana liked those goofy animated features because they were well made and funny, and they took her back to when she was still a little girl. But then, she recognized the dad in the family. He was a tall and distinguished man who was there with his very pretty wife and their two kids who looked to be around 7 or 8.

That tall man was one of Dana's favorite professors from the previous year. His name was Professor Hill, and Dana often felt weird having a crush on him. He was probably old enough to be her grandfather, but he was dressed so elegantly and spoke with a deep and sensuous voice when he gave his classes. That voice often drove many of the co-eds crazy, and Dana was not immune to it either.

The lights went down and the previews started on the screen. Dana was alone in the dark again as she liked to be. But instead of watching the screen, she could not take her eyes off of Professor Hill. The light from the movie illuminated his face in all kinds of colors, and he often turned to talk to his children or whisper to his wife. When he did that, Dana could see his face perfectly even though he had no idea she was watching him.

The urge came on her before she knew it was gathering inside her. As she looked at the face of the older gentleman, Dana began to move her hand on her left thigh. She fell into a dreamy state caressing herself while admiring that handsome older professor just a few yards away. In her thoughts, Dana was feeling that handsome gentleman tenderly moving his hand up her leg.

The happy sounds of the family movie filled the small theatre, and Dana let her thoughts and fingers drift. Soon, she was pushing the hem of her cute skirt up. A deep sigh came from Dana's mouth, but it was not heard because of the movie. She let her fingers slide up her thigh to the rim of her panties. She felt the tingle of excitement in her pussy because of her inappropriate thoughts about Professor Hill and the naughtiness of staring at him and starting to masturbate.

Dana slid the fabric of her panties aside and let her fingers find the familiar folds of her moist pussy. Looking at that handsome face, she let those fingers pleasure her clit and stroke the delicate areas of her open pink pussy slit. Dana was in a wonderful state of euphoria as she slowly masturbated about that handsome man. But then, she suddenly realized that just as she was watching him silently, she was being watched.

Dana did not want to move so she could cover up what she was doing. Then she spotted the person who was spying on her as she spied on the professor. He was little more than a shape in the shadows. But Dana's eyes were sharp in the dark when she recognized the shape of one of the ushers who was standing near the steps of the balcony.

In the moments of the search, she had let her skirt fall back in place. But then, she realized that the boy was not in the business of stopping her. He himself had unzipped his uniform pants, taken out his erection, and begun masturbating looking at Dana. At first, she was shocked but as her eyes adjusted, she could see the shaft of his cock sticking out and his hand moving up and down on it.

Soon, Dana realized he was not going to come over or report her. He was doing what she was doing, but the object of his lust was her legs and pussy. This ignited a new level of excitement in Dana, and she lifted her leg and put it over the arm of the theatre chair. This forced her thigh apart and then she looked away so the boy did not know it was for his benefit and pulled her skirt up to give him a good view.

Dana was very aware of the eyes of that usher on her wet pussy. She pulled the crotch of her panties aside, reached down, and parted the lips so he could masturbate to her pussy with a very erotic view of it. Dana was caught up in what was happening, and she began to stroke her clit.

Faster and faster, she masturbated watching the body of that usher hunch over and beat off to her. Just then, she heard his groan and looked to his hard cock. In the dim light, she saw the stream of cum fire from his cock and land on the chair.

Pushing the Envelope

Dana thought a great deal about the episode with the usher. As soon as it was over, he disappeared. She never got a clear look at his face, but she felt she narrowed down who it was from body type. But he never said anything about it, and she was happy to leave it an anonymous moment in the dark as well. That kept things exciting.

The mutual masturbation session changed how Dana viewed her hobby of going to the movies alone. Suddenly, she yearned for more contact. But to keep it anonymous and not let it become anything out of control was important for some reason. When she went to the movies alone, she felt a wild part of her wanting to take over. She picked another family movie thinking that would keep things under control. Dana went to the balcony but very quickly it filled up with families and children. As she sat there, a family of four came in and they sat down right next to her.

The dad of the family sat next to her and Dana saw him quickly glance at her sexy legs that were easy to admire in the short skirt she was wearing. Because it was a movie that had a lot of action, more people were in the balcony than the floor. So when the movie was about to start, the two children of the couple begged to go down and sit close to the screen. The mom said yes and the children rushed down the steps, which filled up the lower level with excited children and teenagers. In fact, all that was left in the balcony were Dana, the dad next to her and his wife next to him.

It was a little awkward sitting so close, but Dana felt a surge of excitement each time the dad glanced down at her leg. She could also tell his wife was aware he was looking at a girl who was probably half his age. The movie started and the noise of excited children was overwhelming. Dana looked down and saw the man's hand on his leg nearest hers and it was gripping that leg firmly. He was feeling an internal battle that he may not have been winning.

Dana slowly slid her hand down her thigh until it was parallel with his. Then in an act of boldness that was greater than she had ever tried, she slipped her pinkie finger over and looped it through his. Then Dana looked at his face. He was quite handsome although the concern for what was happening was clear. His wife was stunningly pretty with a wholesome look of a Sunday school mom. Yet her long soft blond hair and her perfectly rounded face made it clear that she was quite a prize for this dad to have for the mother of his children.

The husband did not push Dana's fingers

away. Just then, his beautiful wife saw the fingers toying with each other. She gripped his arm but did not speak. Her eyes were glued to what was happening. He was breathing rapidly form the stress, but instead of pulling away, he wove all of his fingers into Dana's hand and held it as if they were on a date. The wife's eyes were glued to what was happening between her husband and Dana.

Dana was on fire with the danger and excitement of this bold step she had taken to push the envelope. Under the wife's watchful eye, she pulled his hand to her leg and moved the fingers from her own fingers to her thigh. The feel of the young girl's warm firm thigh in his fingers drove Elliot beyond control. As Susan looked, her husband began to move his hand up the sexy thigh of the young woman in the next seat. Nothing like this had ever happened to either of them, but the thing that shocked Susan the most was that she did not put a stop to it.

Susan watched her husband push Dana's skirt up revealing more and more of her sexy leg as it came into view. None of the three were watching the movie. Dana was wiggling with excitement at this violation of her body that she brought on. She watched the wife's eyes grow wide as her husband played with Dana's leg and slid his hand all the way to her panties.

Feeling bold, suddenly Dana pushed her hips up and began to wiggle out of her panties. She heard this stranger who was feeling up her legs gasp and under his breath moan "oh god" when he saw Dana's naked pussy within inches of his moving hand. At the same time, his wife leaned over and gazed into the pussy of the young woman. Susan was going wild with crazy emotions and seeing the open cunt of a very sexy young girl only scrambled her insides all the more.

As Susan watched, her husband moved his fingers into the slit of this stranger girl that was seducing both of them. He parted the slit, felt up the pink flesh to her clit, and began to play with it expertly. Dana gasped and held on to the arms of the theatre seat as her sex responded to the stroking the husband was giving to her clit.

Susan felt her own pussy tingling with excitement at all that was going on, and she could no longer just sit and watch. Acting on instinct, she unzipped Elliot's pants and pulled out his rock hard cock. The one thing she knew Elliot always wanted her to do was to suck his cock, and now, it seemed there was nothing that was behind the limits. Susan leaned over and slid the head of her husband's cock into her mouth.

All three were wiggling and moaning, quietly trying not to draw attention to themselves. Dana reached into her purse and pulled out a hand towel. She needed it because just as Elliot slid his index finger deep into her pussy hole, Dana orgasmed hard. She bit down on that towel to muffle her moans of pleasure.

When Elliot felt the young girl cum on his

finger, he was overwhelmed and he arched up and shot his load into his beautiful wife's mouth. Susan felt the surge of hot cum in her mouth and all she could think was to reach down for something to help her contain the flow. She found Dana's panties, brought them up to her lips, and caught the ooze of white sperm that surged from her mouth as her husband finished his orgasm.

The Letter

Dana reflected on the wild threesome that just sort of happened at the movie theatre, and each time she remembered it, it made her touch herself until she orgasmed again. When it was done, Dana headed to one exit and the couple to the other and they did not see each other again. Dana did not finish the movie, but she assumed the couple returned after they settled down and cleaned up so they could collect their kids.

A week later, Dana returned to the theatre with some hesitation, and as she entered the seating, an usher approached her. From his posture and that knowing look in his eyes, she determined it was the one who masturbated looking at her. He did not say a word, but he handed her an envelope and left her in the empty theatre to read it. Dana opened the envelope and read the letter. It read:

"Dear Dana,
I am Susan. You and my husband, Elliot,

had a sexual experience in this theatre the last time you were here. Do not be concerned. I am not angry with you. It opened new worlds for both of us, and our sex life has been amazing since it happened. I learned your name from this usher in the theatre who seemed to know about you.

Dana, that was the most amazing experience either of us have ever had. You should know that we have always been very modest people, and that day was the first time I had sucked my husband off. It has not been the last time. It is also important to say to you that while we treasure what we all shared that day, it cannot happen again. We have not learned any more about you and we will not seek to know it. We want you to forget us too so we can lead lives without fear of guilt. We will never forget you but this must be goodbye.

We will never frequent this theatre again. If you see us in public, please do not greet us. Let that one amazing moment in this theatre always be a magical time we all shared. Speaking for my husband and myself, we want only the very best for you. You are a very special young woman.

With thanks,

Susan."

Dana folded the letter and put it in her purse. She got up from her regular seat and walked down to the floor area. This felt right because as she sat there thinking about all that happened, lots of people filed in around her. Susan picked a movie that was for her age group because now she associated children's features with what happened. The movie that was playing in that theatre was a action adventure genre with lots of comedy, so that was a perfect way to take a break from all the wild activity she had been part of in the balcony.

But just as the screen sprang to life with sneak previews, Dana had an intuition to look back at the entrance. There, standing looking at her in a pretty floral dress and her blond hair made up perfectly was a lovely woman in her early 30s. It took a moment and then Dana gasped to recognize that it was Susan. She caught Dana's eye and then turned her head without smiling and walked up toward the balcony.

Dana stood up and watched the slender figure make her way toward the upper rows of the balcony and sit down on the back row. That was a row that had extra leg room, and it was very dark back there. Dana was nervous, but like a powerful force, she felt drawn to go to that lone woman. She walked up the steps to that back row where they were alone. Susan looked at her with soft eyes and a serious but peaceful expression.

Dana sat down and looked into the eyes of the woman who wrote that letter. "Susan I..." she started to say, and the pretty lady put her finger on her lips. She just shook her head to communicate without words and let the mystery remain forever. Then leaning over nervously, Susan kissed Dana on the lips.

Neither girl had ever kissed another woman with passion before, but the excitement of that kiss swept them both away. Using what they knew from kissing men, Susan slid her tongue into Dana's mouth and Dana sucked it lovingly. Dana felt along Susan's ears and neck and down to her shoulders. Then with some hesitation, she put a hand on the married woman's breast and squeezed it softly.

Susan gasped feeling the young girl feel her tit and she moaned softly breaking their kiss. Then she pulled Dana to her, buried her face in Dana's hair, and kissed down her neck sucking and biting as she went. Dana held her head and stroked her hair. She was dizzy with the newness of it all and how exciting it was to make love to a woman. Susan slipped out of her seat and to the floor in front of Dana.

Eagerly, Dana opened her legs and pulled up her skirt as Susan started kissing her legs and stroking that soft skin that her husband had experienced. When Susan saw that Dana's panties were soaking wet from arousal, any hesitation about performing sex on a girl vanished. She reached up and pulled Dana's panties down to her knees and then leaned over them and buried her face in her pussy. The smells and tastes of Dana's sweet wet cunt were like a drug to Susan as she lapped at her slit and clitoris. Suddenly, Dana grasped Susan by the hair and moaned to feel her orgasm hit just as Susan began to push her tongue into her vagina. The orgasm surged into Susan's mouth filling it with the moisture of Dana's climax.

The two women could not get enough of each other. Susan knelt on the seat of the theatre chair facing away from the screen. Dana turned around also and lifted the skirt of that pretty dress over her hips. When she pulled Susan's panties down, the pretty cunt of the young mother was pouting, wet, and ready for Dana to love it. Dana leaned forward standing up and kissed Susan on the ears and neck as she thrust her fingers into her pussy feeling the round cunt lips and sliding her finger into her wet hole.

With her thumb stimulating the married woman's clit and then two fingers fucking in and out of her vagina, Susan's orgasm came quickly. The movie was keeping the rest of the audience well distracted so Dana and Susan could kiss and finger each other for over an hour. When it was done, Susan kissed Dana softly and slipped out of a door in the back of the theatre.

The Stranger

The letter that Susan had written spoke of Dana never seeing Susan or Elliot. But Susan could not keep that vow, and before long, Dana was invited to their home and even met the children. When those precious kids went to bed, the three explored new levels of excitement in the married couple's bed.

Dana's life had changed so much just because she loved to go to the movies by herself. With the new excitement of Susan and Elliot in her life, Dana did not enjoy her little hobby that often. One cold and dreary Tuesday, Dana felt the desire to enjoy a quiet hour or two in the dark once again. She found her way to the movie theatre where so much had happened.

The theatre was almost empty as Dana sat in the balcony thinking about so much that had happened. When the movie started, it was a slow-moving mystery that put Dana in a strange mood. Just then, she was aware that she was being watched again. She thought it was the usher but it was not. On the other side of the theatre was a tall man shrouded in darkness. The figure moved slowly and smoothly toward the back of the theatre. His slender form created a silhouette of darkness against darkness.

Dana stood and moved toward the figure as though drawn. The shape of the man's body seemed so familiar, but she could not make out his face because the movie was so drab that little light was coming from it. As she got within a few rows of him, she heard a very low voice speak almost in a whisper. It just said her name, "Dana."

Even when Dana reached the figure, she could not see his face. Strong hands turned her and pushed her forward so she had her hands on the back of the chairs and her butt toward the man. He handled her body possessively but gently. Still, she felt she could not deny him. She felt his hands find the hem of her skirt and lift it. He laid the skirt over her butt and without slowing, pulled her panties down to her knees.

Dana wanted to speak and know who was molesting her. At the same time, the excitement of being taken by someone so dark and demanding was overpowering. She was instantly oozing wet and ready to let him penetrate her. She did not have to wait long. The lanky body leaned into her, and she felt the warm skin of a hard penis moving forcefully along the inner folds of her sex. Skilled fingers parted her pussy lips and that hard cock found its home to enter her cunt with a forceful lunge.

Dana found herself lifting her butt and pushing back against the strangers hips as he fucked in and out of her slowly and steadily. He held her around the waist and filled her insides with his large, rock hard cock. All Dana could hear was a soft rhythmic moan of "uh uh uh" as he thrust into her tight hole over and over. Just then, she felt his face on her neck and his lips kissing and sucking her shoulder. She glanced back to see who was fucking her.

When she saw that face, the shock of it sent a quiver through her body. The distinguished lines and grey hair of her Professor Hill made eye contact with her. He kissed her mouth and with one huge thrust shot a volcano of cum deep in his student's hole. Dana wanted to speak to him, but she just put her head back and moaned loudly feeling the powerful eruptions of hot cum inside her. She orgasmed so hard that she doubled over and went to her knees. For several moments, she was out of it and unable to keep up on the world around her. But when she woke up, he was gone. She was once again, alone, filled with her own wet and his load of cum and alone, in the dark.

11 KEEPING A PROMISE

Prologue

Hilary had always been very status-conscious. Victor made a great living with his jewelry store so he could afford to outfit her in the finest of clothing and accessories. She loved that moment when every head turned, and she could almost hear the gasp of how great she looked. She had a lot to work with; before she became a trophy wife, Hilary had been a model. With her jet-black hair, her tall and shapely body, and her long and sexy neck, she drew men to her like a magnet. Victor liked how much men desired her. He did well at keeping her happy with a lifestyle that she enjoyed and that was enough for her.

Hilary belonged to all the right clubs and went to all of the social events that mattered. They attended the church that all the society people were part of, and she was active in civic organizations that gave her plenty of status. Hilary knew that how great she looked helped her husband's status.

But she did not feel he returned the favor. She was not repulsed by his weight for her own right, but she was embarrassed to go out with him because of it. It was an obsession that she could not let go of.

It was a tea that she attended with many of her socialite friends that gave Hilary a plan. Gwen, Joan, and Becky had been close friends with Hilary since they all attended the most expensive schools on the east coast. So the idea of getting down to the nitty gritty of sexual matters was not uncommon at these teas. That was why they always reserved a private room.

"It isn't enough that he shows me off at his executive retreats and lands big deals with his gorgeous wife," Gwen observed, "but then he has the nerve to want sex from me." All of the girls roared at that statement. Of course, it was an overstatement; when Gwen got home, she and her husband Roland had a very creative sex life. But she loved to make the girls laugh.

"I think husbands get all kinds of perverted ideas like oral sex and fantasies when they get on the Internet," Becky chimed in. "I told Steven not to bring any of that nonsense to our bedroom. He is very good though. Get on, get off, and it is over with."

"Well, girls," Joan said with a coy smile. "I have found that sex makes a great bargaining chip. I have given my Larry a few of those pleasures you just mentioned, Becky," she said with a grin, "but he has to pay the price for that first and my prices are high."

The Price Is Right

As Hilary and Victor got ready for bed that night, she thought about what the girls had talked about. It was sex night according to the calendar. Victor seemed to go along with this organized approach even though the spontaneity was not there. Sex took place in bed after all chores were done and both had showered completely. Victor knew the drill.

He approached his wife from behind. She lay facing away and often laid her head on the pillow so she did not face him as he fucked her. In order to get an erection, she allowed him to see her pussy. He was allowed to pull down her nightie bottoms and panties. She had a tremendously sexy body, and this ritual alone made him wild with excitement.

Victor pulled his wife's garments down and he saw the bulge of her sexy pussy that was only for him. The lips of her cunt were perfectly round and covered with a fine black hair. He enjoyed gazing at her beautiful ass and even touching it softly as he prepared to fuck his wife. Victor found the lubricant they used. Because there was no fondling, he had to make his cock slick before sliding it inside her.

He applied the lubricant and eased forward, letting the head of his cock push her pussy lips apart. The pink slit and opening were there for him to enter. Hilary would make slight girlish "ohs" as he began to penetrate her. Inch by inch his cock entered her and he felt the warmth of the inside of her body take it all inside. She remained still and stoic to be fucked, which was both troublesome and erotic to Victor.

He did not lay on her but he pushed up with one arm and thrust his hard cock in and out of her again and again and again. This time he touched the cheeks of her ass and spread them until he saw her anal opening. That was just enough to finish him, and he shot his cum inside her and then pulled out.

Hilary and Victor did not have an unloving marriage. It was just a disciplined one. Hilary was not as frigid as she wanted her husband to think she was. She had never orgasmed when he was inside her, but she had touched her clitoris while he fucked her. And there were those private times in the sauna or in bed alone when she would think of a sexy servant or movie star and manipulate her clit until that overpowering feeling of orgasm took her over. She always felt guilty about it because she would not cum for her husband. But it felt so good to masturbate.

The next day Hilary thought about what Joan said about giving her husband more for a price. Hilary was curious about having a more exciting sex life. But she wanted Victor to earn it. So she crafted a plan. It was the next day that she got a chance to talk to him.

"Victor, are you happy with what we did last night?" she asked. Her tone was friendly and open to talking. "Is the sex what you want?"

Victor thought about the question. "Well, darling," he started, "There are other things I would like. I don't go to other women, so I want to try them with you." He spoke honestly without any hint of demand in his tone.

"Victor, there is something I want very much." Hilary said. "I want you to lose weight and be the gorgeous man I married. I want this and you want more from us, sexually. So let's set a goal. Each time you reach a goal of losing weight, the reward is something new." Victor thought it over for a while and she waited patiently.

"That is a fine plan, my dear." He agreed. "For our first goal, I promise a target of losing ten pounds. And for the reward, I want to make love to you with you on your back facing me. I want you to kiss me with passion and I want to lick you between your legs."

"Done," Hilary agreed, without really thinking about what he had asked for. She was feeling nervous but victorious. She would get her husband in shape so she would feel proud to walk into any public gathering with him. The payoff was a handsome trophy husband to show off at any gathering and for that, she was willing to take the risk.

Goal No. 1

When Hilary looked at the results of the experiment to make her husband conform to her will, it was a smashing success. Victor hit the diet and exercise programs like a man possessed. They used a scale that had been in the master bathroom for years as the way to monitor the weight loss. Within a week, the weight was falling off and Victor was starting to look and feel better.

Each time Hilary recorded his weight loss, she could tell his excitement about collecting his "prize" was growing. Hilary knew that he was going to hit that goal, and she was just as nervous as he was excited. Because he was so aggressive in his diet and workout programs, that 10 pounds fell off in just over two weeks.

When Hilary saw that her husband had hit his first weight loss goal, it was time to set an evening for him to enjoy the rewards of his hardwork. They picked the following Friday night as that was a scheduled sex night for them anyway. The afternoon of the big event, Hilary could not stop thinking about what her husband wanted to do to her. She had always viewed sex as a duty, like cooking or cleaning. That is why she just laid there and just let him stick it in until he released. It was her job. Now she was trying to change that view.

When bedtime came, it was not like the other nights. She did not go get in bed and just lay on her side to offer her vagina to him to fuck. Before she even went to the bed, Victor approached her. She tried to object because a panic feeling came over her. She whispered, "Victor, I..."

But she did not finish the words. He kissed her mouth as if they had never kissed before. Hilary did not know how to respond, but her husband was so commanding and strong that she just melted into his arms. He had included weight training in his workouts, and it was obvious that his muscles were becoming very firm and manly.

Victor kissed her deeply and she felt his lips open and his tongue caress her lips. As though by instinct, Hilary opened her own lips and she tasted the wet of her husband's mouth. The kiss became deep and sensual as Victor slid his tongue into her mouth, exploring it deeply. When Hilary let her own tongue slip into his mouth, he sucked it lightly. She nearly went crazy with excitement and nervousness.

Victor became the very spirit of romance, gently guiding his beautiful wife to their bed. Tenderly he undid her nightgown and let it fall to the floor. Hilary felt nervous and exposed standing naked in front of her husband. Then he pulled his T-shirt over his head and dropped his underwear. When Hilary saw her husband's penis, she blushed. She rarely saw it in lovemaking as he usually mounted her from behind.

She stared down at it as though hypnotized. Victor saw his wife's eyes on his half-hard cock, and he took her soft fingers and brought them forward to wrap around it. As Hilary felt the shaft up and down, it become stiff and bulging in her hand. Victor lowered her to the bed and made sure she laid facing up. Hilary started to roll over to let him approach her from the back, but he wouldn't allow it.

Victor laid the slender and perfect body of his sexy wife on the bed and sat up gazing at her with desire. He reached down to her knees and parted her legs, so the folds of her neatly trimmed pussy were easily visible to him. Her face was bathed in the soft light of the room, but he could see the nervousness and desire in her eyes. She had the look of a schoolgirl about to lose her virginity.

He knelt between her parted legs with his rock-hard cock ready to fuck this beautiful woman. First, he leaned in and kissed her deeply, pulling her to him. She moaned in his mouth and when he began to kiss her neck, she could not stop herself from gasping "Oh yes, Victor."

Victor sucked his wife's neck and felt her round breasts with his hand. Then he forgot himself and said something to her that he had never said. "Hilary, I want to fuck you so bad." He moaned and she gasped loudly at the profanity. Victor was on fire for her. He kissed down to her breasts, licked them, and gently sucked her nipples. Just then, his fingers slid into her pussy and parted the lips. He felt up and down her slit and found her clitoris.

Hilary's back arched with surprise at feeling him fondle her most intimate places. "Oh god...," she moaned as Victor kissed down her stomach toward her open pussy. Hilary remembered he had said he wanted to lick her there, but she never thought it would actually happen. But as he pushed her thighs apart and let his lips go from her belly button to the top of her slit, it happened.

Victor had read about how to give his wife oral sex in preparation of this moment. But until he tasted the musty wetness of her very aroused pussy, he had no idea how it would be. He licked her slit to her pussy hole and up to her clit where he began to lick it and blow on it. His wife responded with wild moans and gasps at what she was feeling. Victor continued to stroke the wet clit, licking and sucking her pouty pussy lips all the way down her cunt. Then he licked the opening to her sex, tasting the wetness that was pouring out of it.

He felt the urgent need to fuck his wife. He was so in love with being so close to her open cunt. Then he saw the tiny puckered opening to her ass. Giving in to temptation, Victor licked down his wife's private areas and began to lap at the rim of that hole. Hilary was almost in orbit from having her cunt eaten out for the first time, but when she felt her butt being licked, it was more than she could endure. "Please, Victor."

Victor pushed himself up to his knees and moved forward like a stalking beast to get inside his wife. He lowered himself on her, supporting himself with his elbows, and reached down to move his stiff cock into position. Hilary forgot all about the lubrication he usually used and instinct took over. She lifted her hips to take his cock and slipped the full shaft inside her wet pussy.

The fucking was fast and needy as Victor took his wife as if it was the first time. In many ways it was.

"Oh God, Victor. Yes," Hilary gasped. She never knew it could be like this. She thrust back up to him, grinding her clitoris into his pelvic bone each time he pounded his cock into her. Suddenly she moaned and screamed all at once and reached her orgasm. She came with a power that made her see colors just as Victor buried his cock deep inside his wife and pumped massive shots of cum into her quivering body.

Twenty More Pounds

It took a couple of days for Hilary to get her wits about her after the wild sex that came out of the first challenge. So much about it was new and exciting. She had been taught that the woman just laid there and took the man's seed without getting any pleasure. When Victor fucked her from the front, licked her out, and then made her cum, she had more pleasure in those few minutes than in her entire single or married life up to then.

There was no question that there would be no going back. Over the next few weeks, Hilary became a borderline nymphomaniac, dragging her husband on top of her to fuck her hard every chance she got. Of course, for Victor this was a dream come true. After lying next to this amazingly perfect sexual creature and only being allowed to put it in and cum, real sex was like a roller coaster ride every night.

After a couple weeks, Hilary settled down, but she was a changed woman. She liked how Victor looked after losing ten pounds, but it still wasn't perfect. Hilary sought perfection in herself, in her home, in her yard, in her friends, and, especially, in her husband. "Victor," she said one night, "You look so great after losing that extra weight. How would you feel about losing another ten pounds?"

Victor looked up from his paper at his lovely wife. "Is there a reward?" he said with a sly tone to his voice.

"Well, my darling," Hilary said joyfully, "the last reward was even more for me than for you. So what can I do to make you even sexier than you already are?"

"Do you recall when I was licking your

pussy the first time, my love?" Victor asked.

"I will never forget that," Hilary answered.

"For a moment, my tongue went lower than your sweet vagina. It gave some love to that other opening down there," Victor reminded her.

"Is that what you want Victor? Do you want your reward to be that you can lick my anus? I don't understand the appeal, darling, but....." Hilary responded.

"Not just lick...." Victor insinuated. It took a moment for Hilary to understand what he really wanted. Victor smiled when he saw the realization hit her.

"Victor that is so taboo," she complained. "Have you done that with a woman before?" she asked grasping at straws to avoid the commitment.

"Darling, you know I have not done anything with anyone but you," Victor answered truthfully. "And I would not do this with anyone else but you. It's your butt or nobody's, Hilary," he finished.

"Well," Hilary said finding a new tactic. "I will need more than ten pounds for that. That is worth at least 15 pounds." She was sure that would make him ask for something else.

Victor stood up and went to the couch where his wife was sitting, sat down, and kissed her tenderly. Then he nibbled her ear and whispered, "Let's make it twenty." And with that, the deal was done.

This was a wager that Hilary wanted to lose as much as she wanted to win. Just as she saw with the first challenge, Victor took to the task of losing those twenty pounds like a fanatic. He worked out constantly and took to a strict diet. And just as she had seen before, the weight just fell off of him. Each week as he got closer and closer to the twenty-pound goal, Hilary began to try to wrap her mind around the idea of allowing him to sodomize her.

The most noticeable thing about his weight loss was how attractive Victor was becoming with his new shape. His exercise with weights transformed his body, giving him a lean and muscular physique. Hilary noticed how often the other women in their social circles gazed at him. And each week as he became slimmer and more muscular, their sex got better and better. So when he weighed in at twenty-one pounds lighter, Hilary was both terrified and excited about their next new adventure.

Hilary's birthday arrived and when Victor gave her a day of pampering at her favorite spa, she was thrilled. The day went by quickly, with a luxurious massage, time in the whirlpool and sauna, and the kind of tender loving care that always made her feel young and invigorated. Part of the package was a special enema that used a custom mixture and was supposed to relax the body from the inside out. She noticed that her massage seemed to focus much more on her upper thighs, butt, and lower back. She didn't know that Victor had requested those treatments because of his special plans. Her muscles were very limber when she was taken home by rented limo with a glass of wine to round off a wonderful birthday splurge.

Hilary entered her home to find it transformed. The lights were dimmed and there were roses everywhere. On the floor, strings of Christmas lights served as a path to lead her through the house. Hilary was a little giddy from all the wine; she giggled as she followed the lights. When she entered her bedroom, it was filled with flowers and candles going everywhere. Hilary felt a warm glow go through her.

Victor came out of the bedroom wearing a red silk robe hanging open to reveal his incredibly sexy chest and tight abs. He crossed the room, took her hand, and kissed it. "Hello, sexy woman," he said softly. Hilary just giggled. "Tonight we make love to fill you with excitement and to satisfy all of your senses. Then you give me the prize for all my hardwork."

Hilary suddenly gasped. She realized what he meant and that he was preparing her for anal sex. "Victor, I am not sure I can." He did not object but put his finger to her lips and then kissed her. She just melted when his tongue slid into her mouth. He kissed her sensuously on the lips and then down her neck. She melted in his arms and let him enjoy the pleasure of slowly taking off her shirt and bra; he slid her skirt down her thighs to the floor. Kneeling in front of her, he slowly peeled down her panties to reveal her pussy.

Victor leaned forward and teased his wife's cunt with his lips. Hilary had trouble continuing to stand as her hips and legs trembled. She moaned, feeling him suck and lick her clit. When his finger slid into her wet vagina, she felt her excitement mounting.

Hilary pressed Victor's face into her pussy as she moaned. "Take me, darling, all of me. My pussy, my mouth, oh God yes, even my ass." She gasped not believing the words were coming out of her mouth.

Victor laid his wife on the bed and kissed her mouth deeply. As their tongues pressed into each other's lips, he turned her over so she could lean on her arms as he readied her for penetration. Looking at her gorgeous naked ass made him wild with desire. Leaning forward he kissed her neck, her shoulders, and down her back. As he did that, his erection slid along the crack of her ass. Then he reached down and pulled those round cheeks apart to let his hard cock massage the inner flesh of his wife's butt crack.

Hilary was shaking, anxious, and tense. But she felt a new kind of desire, too: a desire to feel him inside her. She arched her butt up to receive him. Victor sat back on his knees and held her gorgeous ass cheeks open looking at that puckered anal hole. He gently leaned down and placed soft kisses on each ass check before bringing Hilary's hands from her sides and placing them on each cheek. Obediently, she held her butt cheeks open for her husband.

Victor took a tube of lubricant and put a generous amount on his fingers. Looking at that gorgeous virgin butt opening, he spread the lubricant up and down his rock-hard cock. Then he took a dab on his index finger and tenderly placed it in the rim of Hilary's anus. Hilary moaned at the coolness of the lubricant.

As Victor worked the lubricant into her anal rim, he slid his other hand under her open hips and found her clit. He massaged her clitoris as his finger pressed inside her butt opening to push the lubricant inside. Hilary gasped, feeling his finger inside her and felt her hips respond to how her husband skillfully worked her pussy to get her aroused.

When her anal rim was ready, Victor leaned forward and mounted his wife. Her breathing was fast and broken as he pressed the head of his cock into her slick, wet anus. "Go slow, darling," she begged. She turned her head and they kissed. The kiss continued as Victor slowly pressed and pushed the head of his cock slowly into her.

Suddenly, the rim surrendered and the head of his cock popped inside his wife's asshole. Hilary gasped. The tightness of his wife's asshole held his cock firmly and did not yield easily as he slowly pressed deeper and deeper up Hilary's ass. Victor could sense her pain and hear her grunting, but he was too full of lust to fuck her deep in her butt hole. Instead of feeling his wife pull back, she was pushing up to take more of his cock deeper in her anal tunnel.

Finally, with half of his cock deep in her butt, Victor began to thrust in and out of her slowly. Hilary moaned feeling the power of his trusts in her tight rectum and gripped the blankets and pillows with white knuckles. The pain was like nothing she had known, but feeling her husband's hard cock so deep in her in this new way was building her orgasm fast. Victor wrapped his arms around her middle and humped deeper into his precious wife's asshole. Each thrust took him deeper and deeper.

As the intensity of the sodomy increased, Hilary's moans of pain turned to gasps of passion. "Yes, yes, yes," she whispered. As he pumped himself into her, one of his hands was massaging her right tit and the other worked down to her pussy and began to stroke her slit and massage her clitoris.

Suddenly, he thrust two fingers deep in her cunt and Hilary felt the power of double penetration. Inside her, Victor pressed his fingers upward and was able to contact his moving cock with his fingers through the thin inner walls of her vagina and anal cavities. That feeling set Hilary off and she orgasmed with a power that almost threw Victor off. Instead, Victor's climax took him over and he drove his cock shaft into her and shot stream after stream of hot cum deep in her anus.

With both lovers finished, they collapsed with him still inside her. He loved the warmth of how her rectum hugged his cock, and she loved the feeling of fullness it all gave her. She leaned back and kissed his mouth lovingly.

"I think I am falling in love with you,"

Hilary whispered. Her admission made him kiss her with deep passion.

Then she whispered playfully, "What will we do for your next 20 pounds."

Victor just smiled and kissed her softly and responded in a soft whisper, "I think we are both satisfied with the weight loss program my love."

"I think you're right, sweet husband." Hilary responded, "I think you're right."

12 STAGE MOMS

Prologue

"**M**an, these spoiled brats are going to kill me!" Ed said to Franklin in the break room. It was a plum gig. Being a cameraman for one of the top-rated teen shows on television meant job security and a fat pay check. The union made sure you went home happy, and since most of these shows run for three or four years minimum, the entire thing becomes routine.

Franklin had worked in movies and in other forms of entertainment, so he had a great reputation as a cameraman. But he hated how each of those gigs ended. When the production wrapped, it was up in the air where or when he would work again. Not only that, but the production values on these simple teenage comedies were never that high. The teenagers and moms and dads that watched just wanted to see the teen star of the month do goofy stuff. So as long as you basically pointed the camera in the right direction, you had it made.

Ida Idaho was the name of the teenage comedy show that Franklin and Ed worked on. It was an outrageous hit. The core of the show was this young girl who was a regular high school girl with a secret identity of Ida Idaho. That secret identity was that of a secret agent who got herself in all kinds of scrapes. She had the help of her brother, Ralph; her dad, Ronnie; and her two best friends forever, Lolly and Miranda.

Because the show had a lot of scenes at the school or at public events, it needed an army of young teenage actors to fill the sets. As a result, the producers were flooded with kids and their stage moms who rushed the studio for just one chance to get a shot at stardom on the show. They came from all over the city by planes, trains, and automobiles from every corner of the country.

Franklin was glad that he often was up above the activity around the set. All those parents and kids created chaos, especially when they were doing auditions, which seemed to be all the time. He usually saw the stage moms who would bring their princesses to the audition. This could take an hour or two if they have to be in a group scene. Then the moms would go to the producer's office to discuss the process of getting a girl on the show and to review contracts. At least that is what he assumed they were reviewing.

The Ida Idaho Show

Julia didn't mind the 3-hour bus ride if it meant the chance for her 13-year-old girl Savannah to try out for the Ida Idaho show. When they watched the show together, Julia felt for certain that her little girl could out perform any one of those regulars on that show. She made sure that Dan, her husband, had everything he needed to get by for a few days taking care of their son. Then, she and Savannah set out to make her a star.

Julia made sure that Savannah was dressed at the height of style for her age. She knew the show well so Julia knew just what to buy. She also dressed very stylishly for the trip to the studio so she would attract attention when it was time to negotiate a contract for Savannah. Julia wore a very stylish top that had ruffles and an expensive skirt that cut off just above the knee and showed off her slender legs nicely.

The first round of auditions went quickly. Savannah was invited to the big studio to audition on the set of Ida Idaho. There were plenty of stage chaperones around sent by the studio. Just then, Julia felt a tap on her shoulder. "Mr Henderson would like to talk to you about signing Savannah," the young woman said.

Julia entered the very nice office and closed the door. Behind the desk was a well-dressed executive. He stood and extended his hand. "Mrs. Johansson, I am John Henderson. May I call you Julia?"

"Of course!" she said, smiling sweetly. She only found one place to sit down. That was a large couch. The cushions were unusually deep. She could not sit back. So she kept a dignified posture looking across at the powerful man. When it was all done, Mr. Henderson turned around and put the paperwork in a folder and on the credenza on top of a large stack of other folders.

"Excuse me, John," she said nervously, "What is that stack?"

"Well, Julia, you saw how many girls are out there to be on Ida Idaho. So this is the stack of contracts we have to pick from. There is a tall stack and a short stack." He said getting up from his desk. He walked over to the couch and stood next to Julia looking down at her.

"I want Savannah to be on that short stack, John." she had a power move to play. John moved his fingers to the top of Julia's blouse that was just at the top of her cleavage. In a relaxed way, he pulled that fabric out and looked down her top at her perfectly formed mommy tits resting comfortably in her dark brown bra.

"That is what every stage mom wants," he said softly. Then he sat down on the couch. He took both sides of her blouse at the shoulders and pulled it down, so her tits were revealed just inside her bra. "And we can move Savannah's over whenever you are ready," he concluded.

When the studio casting director leaned in and began to kiss Julia on the neck, she was in shock. She heard about this kind of thing, but she was just an average housewife. How could this be happening to her? But it was happening to her. Mr. Henderson knew what he wanted. He sucked her neck, reached back, and released her bra. Then he pushed her back onto that big couch that was clearly designed to be used to seduce stage moms.

Julia wanted to say "Please stop!" to the aggressive studio head, but her head was swimming. It all was so smarmy, but exciting at the same time. She felt his mouth reach her tits. Julia just moaned, feeling her nipples being sucked and chewed by John as she lay back. She thought of her daughter not far off doing her audition and her husband at home and still she just moaned and held John's head to her tits.

Julia felt the demanding man push her legs back and force the skirt of her pretty dress up to her hips. He was not to be denied. His intensity, lust, and the way he was just taking her made her tremendously turned on. The producer didn't even take off her panties. He buried his face in her neck, sucked it, and moaned, "I am going to fuck you."

Julia could do nothing but moan, "Oh yes," as he skilfully opened his fly and pulled out his stiff cock. It angled up to push into her wet cunt. He pulled aside the fabric of her panties and that was all he needed. Like it had a homing beam, that hard cock found her vagina rim easily and plunged inside Julia. She gasped and arched up taking the first new cock in her since she got married. She was being molested and she loved it. Within moments, she had a powerful orgasm just as the children's show executive shot a huge load of cum inside her.

The Limo

Franklin paid attention to the non-stop parade of stage moms who went into that office to make arrangements for their princess to be the next star. They were always in there much longer than was necessary and came out with their clothing and hair out of place. Often they forgot their shoes in there, and they usually had that dazed look on their faces like a woman who had been freshly fucked.

Not every stage mom got this treatment. But one thing Franklin noticed is that the daughters of the women who went into those "conferences" really did no better in their progress than the other girls. Each of the girls whose moms "put out" that extra effort got a spot in a crowd scene on the Ida Idaho show. But those spots were rotating and the little girls were often on their way home after one scene on camera and a $35 paycheck to frame showing they were on TV.

It took a lot of organization to manage this army of eager moms and hopeful little girls coming and going from the studio. The audition studio was a separate operation entirely from the show, and it was arranged to have studio workers on hand to guard the young actresses while their moms went to visit the producer unprotected. It put on a good appearance that the young girls really were auditioning for Ida Idaho. Along with that, there was a special limo service that was offered to stage moms to pick up the future stars at the airport and give them the royal treatment to their auditions.

Franklin soon had it figured out that this was a scam that was getting the producers fees they were charging the parents and plenty of pussy on the side. He wanted in on the act. He found a way to moonlight from his cameraman job to driving that limo. It was a sweet gig. The moms knew the ride would cost at least $100. For each mom and young actress that Franklin delivered, he turned over $25 of that to the studio and pocketed the rest.

Franklin picked up a group of three stage moms and their young hopefuls at the airport using the studio limo. The excitement in that car was popping. The barrier was closed between the gals and the driver, but there were hidden cameras that were put there to enjoy the view. As Franklin drove, he switched from camera to camera and enjoyed looking up the skirts of those moms. He was shocked how many of those foxy moms were riding without panties on, and he got nice close up view of their very sexy pussies.

After he delivered the ladies and their daughters to the studio where the "auditions" were held, it was common for a stage mom to approach Franklin. "Do you have any contacts that can help my Katy get noticed?" one mom asked as she handed him the $100. Then she added another $200 to that payment, closed her hand over his, and added, "I will do anything to get Katy on Ida Idaho." Then she made eye contact with him and said in a low voice, "Anything."

Franklin shuddered at her offer of sex because she looked like his best friend's grandma. But the light came on that he had a new opportunity. These stage moms wanted to have their cherubs win at any cost. He worked through the gathering of stage moms and casually mentioned to the mom of the moment that her child had exceptional talent and that he could make a phone call. The "tips" he collected for this extra help varied from another $100 to $1000.

The Scam

The last stage mom he approached looked more like a teenager than a mom. He had spotted her during the ride in because she was slender with wispy blond hair that hugged her face. The color of her hair was almost white, and she looked closer to the age of the young actresses than to the age of most of the stage moms. Checking her nametag, Franklin learned her name was Lexi, and by looking at the records, she was there with her sister Amber. Franklin felt his heart leap that Lexi was only 23.

"Amber is so talented." Franklin said after he worked his way through the stage moms to stand next to Lexi. The look on her sweet, perfectly shaped face was priceless.

"Do you think so?" Lexi whispered. "Can you help her get through this mob of girls who are auditioning?" she asked with a sincere look in her eye. "You drove us in didn't you?"

"Yes," Franklin whispered. "I do some pre-screening during this stage so that only the best girls get to the second round of auditions. I think Amber has what it takes." Lexi gasped and suppressed a squeal of delight that she may be able to help her sister make it to the big time.

"So what do we do to get her to that stage?" Lexi whispered grasping Franklin's arm possessively.

"Let me make a phone call. Come with me in case I need any information." Franklin said softly. He took her hand and led her to an empty office. He felt like he was stealing her away, but the longer he looked at her, the more he wanted Lexi all for himself. He escorted Lexi into that room, closed the door, and locked it so there would be no interruptions. Franklin gestured toward the couch and pretended to make a phone call.

He was quite the actor pretending to be

talking to the hiring manager for Ida Idaho. "Leo, I tell you this Amber has what we need for the show. So what do I need to get her out of this crowd of no talent brats?" Lexi was squirming on that couch in excitement. Then he covered the speaker of the phone. "There are some costs involved with skipping this step but they are not bad." He whispered.

"I have $1000 Franklin. Is that a good start?"

"We can bring $1000 over in about an hour Leo." He spoke into the dead phone. Franklin held out his hand toward Lexi. "Yes, I have that much in my hand from her sister right now."

That was all it took. Lexi got into her purse, produced the cash in a snap, and handed it over to him. The scam was going perfectly.

"Great, Leo! We don't want to raise anyone's curiosity. We have about an hour left on this part of the audition. I will bring her right over after that."

He laughed at a pretend joke that Leo said on the other end. Of course, there was no Leo.

Franklin pretended to end the call and then looked at Lexi and said in low voice, "It's all set up." Lexi was so thrilled she jumped up and ran to Franklin and gave him a huge hug. Then without taking her arms away, she looked up into his eyes. Franklin did this as a scam but his heart melted looking at the gorgeous girl. He kissed her softly and sweetly.

That kiss quickly turned deep and sexy and he guided her to the couch. This was the first stage mom he seduced, so his heart was about to blow up in his chest. He lowered her to the couch kissing her neck down to her shoulder. She moaned and stroked his hair as he took her on that couch. He didn't know how much time he had so Franklin began to pull up Lexi's skirt. "Oh god!" he heard her say in a whispered gasp but she did not fight him. Instead, she pulled it up more and whispered, "Hurry."

He had to hurry because he was sure he was going to cum too soon. He unzipped his pants as the stage sister pushed her panties down. They were not even all the way down when Franklin pushed her thighs apart and moved his hard cock into her slit, feeling the warmth and wet of her sex on it. When he found her hole, instinct just took over.

Franklin surged forward letting every inch of his very hard penis press into her inch by inch. The young girl held onto the clothing on his back and his hair, pushing her hips back to take all of his cock. Sliding his hands down to her hips, he reached around, took one slender butt cheek in each hand, and grasped it tightly. Then he started to fuck her. At first, the thrusts were slow and deep and then the movement became rapid and demanding.

"Fuck me!" Lexi gasped and that was all it took. He buried his hard cock completely inside her and came in six or seven massive spurts of hot sperm.

When it was done, he stayed inside her for a minute or two. Then he kissed her and whispered, "Let's make your sister a star." They got dressed and rushed out of that private room. She was excited about his promises little knowing they were all lies.

The Moms

Franklin did not see much of Lexi after that, but she and her sister were around. It turned out that Amber was very talented and she got spotted by a legitimate agent of the Ida Idaho show. So she enjoyed some success. One afternoon Franklin was grabbing a bite to eat at the studio cafeteria when he saw Lexi and Amber having lunch too. He swung by and greeted them.

As he began to leave their table, Lexi stood up and hugged him. "You kept your promise," she whispered in his ear and she kissed his cheek. Franklin blushed and went on feeling a rare flash of guilt. But it passed quickly.

Franklin perfected the scam so it prospered him in every way. He learned to gather more and more "fees" - both from the moms who were being shuttled to the studio and from those who got his private services. If Franklin had wanted to keep count of how many sexy stage moms he took into his private chambers, billed money out of, and then fucked silly, he couldn't count that high.

The day came when Franklin had the chance to take on a new challenge in his little scam operation. As he escorted the stage moms and the youthful actresses to the audition stage, he greeted two women who clearly were traveling together. As Franklin showed the group around, Franklin stayed close to those two women and their daughters. The women were stunning despite the fact that they were probably in their late 30s.

It did not take much to get the moms to tell their stories. The taller of the two had jet-black hair that she wore over her shoulders. Her figure was slender and round but not buxom. Her name was Jill. The shorter wore her brown/red hair to her neck and curled under her jaw on both sides. She was shorter and had a much more noticeable roundness to her breasts and hips. She was not fat but everything about her was all woman. Her name was Ursula.

Ursula and Jill had been lifelong friends. They married twin brothers so technically they were sisters-in-law. They had their daughters on the same weekend, so the babies were side by side in the nursery. Ursula's daughter was named Hope and Jill's was named Faith. The cousins were inseparable friends, and they looked like twins because of their genetic bond through their dads.

The two stage moms brought the girls to Ida Idaho to audition together. They were certain that if the producers saw how adorable and talented Faith and Hope were, they would invent two new roles to take a prominent part in the show. They poured their story out to Franklin as they rest of the party went on ahead, and the little girls were taken to the audition stage to get their makeup done and work with their coaches.

"I think the idea of a new set of roles for Faith and Hope is an amazing idea." Franklin lied to the two gorgeous stage moms. "My job is to do a little pre-screening as the girls are being checked in, and I think I can put in a good word for them and get the paperwork started to get them on the show."

Ursula and Jill jumped like two teenagers at the idea of working a behind the scenes deal to get their girls ahead of the pack. They just didn't know how behind the scenes it was. Franklin escorted those crazy hot women to that private office where he fucked so many stage moms. But this was the first time he took two of them in there.

Franklin staged the phone call the same way he did with Lexi and all of the other women. It was late in the day so it was dark in the small room, so Franklin turned on a lamp and looked at those two very fuckable women as he finished the fake phone call. As he ended the call, he said, "Let me see if they would be able to work that out." Then he walked over to that couch and sat down between Ursula and Jill.

"Well ladies, it is practically in the bag," he said in low tones and with that he put one hand on Jill's leg and the other on Ursula's and rubbed them slowly. "I can see how your daughters became so gorgeous with such sexy moms."

Ursula was all for it and she started rubbing Franklin's leg moving her hand up toward his rapidly stiffening cock in his pants. But Jill was nervous. "Is this part of the deal?" she said as Franklin's hand slid up under her skirt. "We are married women, not sluts," she continued.

"No, no ladies." Franklin assured them. "Faith and Hope's talents are all that is needed and the deal is in the works. I can be a help for them every step of the way." He said leaning over and kissing Ursula's neck. Ursula made eye contact with her best friend and sister-in-law and mouthed "Its ok" to her and then she took Jill's hand and put it on Franklin's crotch where the zipper was.

Jill was reluctant but she noticed the big bulge in his pants. She missed her husband and that hard cock was hard to resist. She slowly unzipped his pants and pulled open the fly. Then Ursula reached in and pulled out Franklin's hard cock so both women would enjoy stroking the shaft, the moist head, and his balls.

Ursula turned her face to his and kissed Franklin's mouth passionately. Then she whispered, "What did you need to work out?" Franklin sat up and gazed in to the faces of these two stunning creatures. Then he went for it.

"Well, he wanted to assure that the girls could play twins and that they were very close. I assured him that I could tell their moms were very very close." He said softly. He extended his finger to Jill's lips and touched them lightly. Then he took that finger and touched it to Ursula's lips as a type of kiss.

It took a moment and then the moms realized what he was suggesting. He leaned in and sucked Jill's neck as Ursula looked down at Jill's hand wrapped around his cock. Ursula reached over and felt up that sexy hard cock letting her fingers intertwine with her best friend's fingers. The two friends were nervous about crossing the lesbian line with each other but so turned on, they gave in. They began to kiss furiously as their fingers played with Franklin's hard cock.

As Jill rolled on top of Ursula kissing her deeply, Ursula pulled open her blouse to get to her friends small sexy tits. That is when Franklin pushed up Jill's skirt over her slim butt cheeks and pulled down her panties to get inside her.

When Jill felt Franklin ram his stiff member into her wet hole, she arched up and moaned. He was the only man to ever be inside her other than her husband, and she gasped at his bigger size than the man she was used to. As Franklin fucked in and out of the stage mom furiously, Ursula leaned in and began to kiss and suck her friend's hard nipples. This was all too much for Jill who had a surging orgasm underneath Franklin.

Jill rolled off of Ursula and Ursula bent down to see her best friend's pussy soaking wet from her climax. That is when Franklin laid down behind Ursula and pulled up her skirt to fuck her deep and hard. When Franklin came inside of Ursula, she was overwhelmed with the amount of his cum that she felt deep in her hole.

This went on for a good 20–30 minutes. It got to where Franklin did not know for sure whose mouth was sucking his cock or who he was inside of at any time. They were a tangle of legs, arms, and naked parts all mixing and making each other cum over and over again. Just then, Franklin heard voices outside the locked door.

Quickly he got himself together and tried to get the dazed stage moms back into shape. Franklin knew this drill having fucked a lot of women in that office. He rejoined the main stage where young actors and actresses were working out the stage direction for the next Ida Idaho episode. Just then, Mr. Henderson made it a point to stand behind him.

"Franklin, I understand you have been helping out with the stage moms."

Franklin's heart froze.

"Yes, sir."

"I understand that you have gathered quite a bit of revenue from those interviews. I trust you will be sharing a small cut of that with management."

The senior producer continued.

"Yes." Franklin agreed, not too worried as he had banked a lot of money that he had scammed the stage moms out of before he fucked them.

"And you have enjoyed the fringe benefits of building relationships with the stage moms."

"Yes, sir." Franklin confessed waiting for the gavel to fall.

"Well, that is the kind of resourcefulness and self-starting attitude we need around here." Mr. Henderson said. "Let's give you a shot at a producer job." He laughed at the shocked expression on Franklin's face.

"It's a better pay check and there is one more thing that comes with it."

He smiled.

"Your own office with a nice wide couch."

Franklin was stunned that he got rewarded for molesting the stage moms. As he walked toward the back of the soundstage, he suddenly found himself looking into the gorgeous eyes of Lexi.

"Well hi, big boy." She said. "How about a big hug for being a hero to me and Amber?"

Franklin forgot about the sex he just had with Ursula and Jill. He hugged Lexi back and kissed her sweetly.

"Oh, I want lots more than a hug. Lots, lots more. Let's get a cup of coffee. I have lots to tell you about."

13 THE GIFT OF LIFE

Prologue

"Come on, big boy. Don't you want to fuck me?" Caroline teased her handsome husband Richard to make him good and horny. She pulled him into bed and pushed his underwear down so she could begin to fondle that nice cock of his. "Oh yes, lover, you have such a sexy cock," she moaned. She was not that good at sexy talk but there was a method to her madness.

Richard began to get into it when he pulled down the tiny nightie top to reveal his wife's cute tits. She was a dainty girl so her breasts were not large. Those sweet mounds turned him on each time he started to kiss and suck them. He could at times get one of her tits entirely in his mouth to suck it and that drove her wild with passion.

Richard's cock firmed up in his wife's tiny fingers as he sucked her nipples and then kissed her mouth. "You want me to fuck you, don't you slut?" He whispered even though the last thing he really thought of his wife was that she was a slut. He wiggled his underwear down so she did not stop playing with his cock. That felt so wonderful, but he knew to be careful he did not cum while she pleased him this way.

"Stick it in me, sexy man," she moaned like a slut. She rolled on to her back and started to slide her panties off. Richard was way ahead of her and as he slipped those tiny undergarments down her sweet sexy legs, Caroline pushed pillows under her butt so her pussy would be pushed up into position for fucking.

Richard looked down on the girl he wooed in their teen years and who was now his wife. She looked up between her open thighs with a loving gaze. Her sexy cunt was open and her sweet pussy hole was ready to be fucked deep and hard. He leaned over her, positioned his hard cock in the rim, and pushed it all the way in to the balls in one thrust. She was oozing with wetness, but still she gasped feeling him plunge his hard manhood into her.

He fucked her steadily, controlling his body so as not to knock her out of that position. Even as he felt the urge to fuck her wildly, he used his arms to position himself and thrust his hard cock to full penetration inside her and then out and back in over and over again. "Yes baby," Caroline moaned, "Fill me up with your sperm!"

That was all it took. Richard leaned in and pushed the entire shaft of his long cock deep inside. His orgasm hit hard and he moaned as he pumped stream after stream of warm cum deep inside her. He held her legs in position and looked down as his testicles constricted and filled her up with the sperm she wanted so they could try to make a baby.

Making a Baby

It wasn't like when they just fucked for fun. The timing and the methods that entered into fucking to make a baby were different. During that short window when Caroline was ovulating, she was a sex machine. She dragged him to bed and begged for his cum constantly. When she got her period, the depression that set in killed sex for weeks only to start the cycle over again.

When he finished pumping his sperm inside his pretty wife, he got up and got her some water as she stayed in position. Caroline always stayed on her back with her hips raised so the sperm inside her could have gravity to help it reach her eggs. She ate right, kept a positive attitude and encouraged her husband in ways to make himself more fertile as well.

But it didn't work. When her period came not long after that, she was very blue.

Richard held his wife in his arms tenderly as she wept from frustration. They had taken all the tests to see if both of them were producing healthy eggs and sperm. Then the report came back that is was Richard who had a low sperm count and that Caroline was fertile and ready to become pregnant.

They discussed all the options. Caroline didn't like adoption because she wanted to give birth to a child that was conceived inside her. For that reason, artificial insemination using a sperm donor was not something she wanted to try. She loved the feeling of her husband pumping sperm into her and the idea of that turning into a wonderful baby touched the future mom in her deeply.

Finally, a plan came up that was unusual and a little scary but would give Caroline the satisfaction of feeling herself become impregnated. They would use the seed of someone else. But it had to be someone they both cared about. They finally decided to ask Richard's best friend Owen to provide the seed. The twist that would take some maturity for everybody involved was the delivery method.

Caroline wanted to be impregnated naturally. That would mean that Owen would have intercourse with her. Richard and Caroline struggled with that side of it and decided it was a loving decision, not cheating because she would not let another man inside her vagina for the purpose of love or orgasm. In fact, Caroline even devised a plan so that Owen could penetrate

her and plant his seed in her womb and not
let it turn into lovemaking.

Make a Baby in Me

When Owen showed up at the home of
Caroline and Richard, his nervousness was
high. Richard greeted him and they talked
for a while in the living room. Richard
wanted him to know that they were both
grateful for what he was about to do. Owen
told him that he felt his wife, Angela, needed
to know. It was hard for her to accept that
her husband would be having intercourse
with Caroline.

Angela finally saw the step as a loving
gesture of friendship. She even cooperated
by planning their own sex life so that Owen
would have a good supply of sperm to
donate when Caroline called for him to come
over because she was ovulating. There were
a number of tears shed as Caroline and
Angela discussed this intimate act of love
and friendship. In many ways, it brought
them all closer together.

"Caroline is in the bedroom, Owen"
Richard informed him. "When you go in, she
would prefer you do not speak. She is lying
on her tummy on the bed with her hips
elevated just right. You will only see her
from the waist down. You will be able to see
her sex area to help you become aroused.
Take your time and be sure to empty your
entire ejaculation in her and leave it in until

you are done so she collects it all. I am going out for a while so you will not feel like I am watching over your shoulder. And thank you so much for this," he finished.

Owen entered the bedroom and closed the door behind him. He tried to be quiet but Caroline heard him come in from the bed. She had a separate sheet over her head and back as she lay face down on the bed. Another sheet was over her legs and butt which were naked. When Owen entered, Caroline pulled the lower sheet away so he would be able to see and have access to the lower half of her body.

Owen approached the bed and gasped when he saw the sexy naked legs and butt of the wife of his best friend. He had always had a secret crush on Caroline and had masturbated about her more than once. But now not only was he going to fuck her, he was a hero for doing so. Inside that sexy and cute body was an egg ready to be fertilized by him. Caroline knew he was staring at her ass. It was the first time any man had seen her naked since she got married. She was both scared and very turned on. Almost by instinct, she opened her legs to let him see her pussy.

Owen tried to be quiet as he took off his clothes. He did not want to be hindered when he got on top of Caroline to fuck her. As he pulled down his pants and shorts, his cock popped out already hard from seeing her lying there seductively. He climbed on the bed and put his hand softly on her ankle at first to let her know he was there. She gasped and a slight shudder of nervousness went through her. Without speaking, he gently stroked her lower leg reassuringly.

Caroline's thighs were parted so Owen's eyes instantly were locked on the soft folds of her pussy. The lips were pouty and covered with a soft mat of hair. Slowly, he moved up between her legs, which pushed her thighs open a little more. Just then, he heard the door to the house close so he knew that Richard had left.

Alone with her, Owen leaned in and touched the lips of her pussy. The gorgeous pink slit appeared to him, but when he saw her sweet sexy vagina opening, he thought he would cum right away. He knew he had to get moving so he could be inside her when his sperm shot out. Owen leaned in and rested his weight on one arm as he held his cock in his fingers to place it in position to drive inside her.

When the head of his cock found the rim of Caroline's opening, both of them gasped and he heard her moan softly.

Owen did not respond. Taking his fingers away, he applied gentle pressure. Her cunt was soaking wet so he knew that she was very aroused by the idea of fucking him. Just then the head slid inside her and with consistent pressure his entire cock pressed inside of Caroline's hole, filling it up.

Because of the danger of cumming too fast, Owen quickly began to fuck her in and out. He was thrilled to feel her respond pushing up and back to take his cock. She was fucking him back. He leaned forward and slid his arm around her to stroke her soft belly.

He knew this was more than she wanted, but he pressed his face into her back that was covered by the sheet. As he felt the warmth and wetness of her insides as he fucked deep into her, he let his fingers slide down to her pussy and find her clit. When he began to stroke it, she moaned. Suddenly, Caroline gasped "oh" and pushed up to Owens thrusting cock. She orgasmed constricting around his cock over and over with her climax. That was all Owen could take and he came inside her.

The load of sperm he pumped into this sexy woman was massive. He just kept cumming and cumming, and every drop of it was shot deep in her wet pussy so it could swim up to her waiting ovaries. When the orgasm finally finished, he laid on her and kissed the fabric on her back. She was breathing deeply but he sensed a soft hum of happiness. When he felt he had been inside her enough, he let his softening cock slip out of her and was about to get out of bed. But before he finished his job with her, he heard a very soft whisper come from under the sheet. Caroline simply whispered lovingly to the first man to fuck her other than Richard, "Thank you Owen."

Spouses

During the week when Caroline was fertile, she wanted to be fucked almost every night. She knew that the sperm from the first night that Owen fucked her stayed active in her system for as long as two days. But to be certain, Owen planned to come back the night after that to repeat the exercise. The problem with that is that it was more than an exercise to Owen, and secretly, it was more than that to Caroline. She did not expect to cum as hard as she did when Owen was inside her. In fact, her orgasm when he was fucking her was more powerful than any she had with her husband.

Everyone felt awkward about what was going on but that was to be expected. But Caroline and Richard talked about it openly so that there was no sneaking around happening. Owen and Angela did the same thing. He did not tell her how turned on he got. Neither Angela nor Richard opened up about buried feelings of jealousy either because the goal of helping Caroline get pregnant was so important.

When Owen came back, Richard greeted him. Caroline was in the bedroom waiting to be fucked. But the men visited for a bit and had a drink so that their friendship had a chance to get some time. Richard did not want to send his best friend into his bedroom to fuck his wife with any guilt. Richard and Caroline were counting on Owen and guilt would not help the process.

Richard got his keys to leave so that

Owen and his wife had their privacy. As he looked back, Owen opened the door to go into the bedroom and Richard glanced at Owen's pants and saw a very pronounced boner. He was very much ready to put that big cock inside his sweet wife's pussy.

Richard went to the car thinking about what was about to happen in that bedroom. He was confused. He was excited about Caroline getting pregnant. He was also upset that she was about to be fucked by another man even if it was someone they both chose. Then there was the most confusing part, he got a little hard on thinking about Owen fucking Caroline.

Just then, his cell phone rang. It was Angela, Owen's wife. "Hi Angela," he answered the phone cheerfully. He was concerned that she was feeling lonely or upset.

"So are they together Richard?" she said in a sad kind of voice. He told her that they were and that he had left the house. "I understand why you feel that way Richard," she said. "You are the only one who understands... I get so confused. But the idea that Owen is about to be inside of another woman is upsetting to me even if it is for such a good reason."

"I feel the same way Angela. That is why I'm out driving around," he answered her.

"I'm about to have dinner. Why don't you come over and we can at least keep each other company," she said with a hopeful sound to her voice. Angela was a good friend and it seemed like a comforting idea to wait this thing out with someone who understood.

Angela was very glad to see him. They talked and had some wine and laughed to forget about what was happening at his house. After they ate, they sat on the couch and laughed, but after a while, they both got quiet knowing that Owen was inside of Caroline by this time.

Finally, Richard turned at looked at Angela. She was a very sexy woman with high cheekbones and well-styled jet-black hair that hugged her face to show off her best features. She was taller than Caroline, and her figure was perfectly shaped to exude a huge amount of sexuality. "What is frustrating, Angela," Richard said, "is that I am not even allowed to make love to my own wife because she only wants your husband's sperm in her. So I am all pent up this week."

"I am the same way Richard. Owen wouldn't even touch me last night because he said he had to store up sperm for Caroline. How does he think that makes me feel?"

"He is a fool not to want to have scx with you, Angela. You are one of the sexiest women I know," Richard said.

"Oh, Richard," Angela said with a soft sigh. "I always thought you were so sexy ever since high school." Both of them knew what was happening, but they felt that they only had each other. So when Richard kissed Angela, they did not feel any guilt about it. He pulled her down onto that couch, thrusting his tongue into her mouth.

Instantly, Richard's hard on was full and aching.

He pulled her down onto the couch, kissing her deeply and then kissing her long sexy neck. "It's happening now, Richard," Angela gasped. "Owen is fucking Caroline right now," she moaned and that drove the two neglected spouses wild. Owen pulled Angela's tank top down to reveal her gorgeous breasts. They were much bigger than Caroline's and her nipples more round and pronounced.

"Oh God, Richard, do it, fuck me." She moaned out of her head with desire. The rational Angela would never think of cheating on her husband, but she wanted a cock in her just like her best friend Caroline had at that exact moment.

Richard didn't need any more encouragement. He pulled up Angela's white skirt and unzipped his pants. Instantly, his big hard cock sprang out and it hit Angela's legs as he pushed his pants down on top of her. Angela moaned feeling Richard's mouth on her tits, kissing and sucking them. She lifted her butt so he could work her panties down enough to fuck her.

"What are we doing?" she gasped pulled his shirt over his head. "This is so wrong." She moaned but then she grabbed his hard cock, stroked it, and guided it to her wet pussy.

Richard drove his hard prick to the balls inside of Angela in one powerful thrust. "Oh yes!" she moaned, feeling her cunt full of hard cock like she wanted. Richard's conscience tried to stop what was happening, but his hips were in motion as he fucked in and out of Angela faster and faster. He reached around and held her butt cheeks, and fucked her furiously on that couch. He was so out of his mind with lust that he pulled open her butt cheeks and felt down the soft crack of her ass.

Owen had never played with her ass like that and Angela gasped with surprise and excitement as Richard squeezed and felt that sensitive flesh with his hard cock fucking her cunt furiously. But when he touched the rim of her butt hole and probed it until tip of his finger slipped inside, she went off like a car bomb. Her orgasms were loud and explosive almost throwing Richard off.

Richard held on to Angela's ass as she came and that put him over the top too. He suddenly surged inside her burying every inch of his cock in her. He shot so much cum inside her he didn't think he would ever stop. When he finally stopped, they fell together, gasped, and kissed.

They agreed this would never be told to anyone. They felt ashamed but as they talked, they both admitted they had never had a better orgasm. Richard stood up to pull himself together. But then Angela leaned forward and took his soft cock in her hand. "Since we have sinned already...," she said kissing the head of his cock. Richard was beyond the ability to resist her when she stood up and walked toward the bedroom lifting her skirt so he could see that sexy ass he had just begun to play with.

The Sheet Comes Off

Owen and Caroline assumed their spouses were waiting faithfully until they finished fucking so they could have time with them. Those spouses were waiting, but not faithfully. Owen entered the bedroom as before, quietly. As soon as he saw the bed with Caroline's legs and butt extended from that sheet, he got hard. He had thought a lot about the feeling of being inside her. It was more than just doing a friend a favor. Fucking his best friend's wife was the most exciting thing he had ever done.

He felt more in control this time. He stood at the foot of the bed and reached down and caressed Caroline's feet before he even took off his clothing. She seemed to be shaking to his touch. Caroline also was nervous their last encounter sent her into waves of orgasms that she had never known before. It bothered her that the feel of Owen mounting her to give the gift of life when he shot her full of cum was even more exciting than she found her husband.

Owen gently pulled Caroline's legs apart as he touched her naked feet until he could see the bulge of her sexy pussy easily. His hard on was bothering him inside his pants so he took his time looking at that sexy cunt he was going to fuck and undressing. When he was naked, he crawled into bed with that hard cock hanging down and began to kiss Caroline's thighs just above the knee.

Caroline shuddered with worry and excitement. If they were doing what they said at first, he would just get on and fuck her and get off. She only wanted to make him excited enough to get hard. But the kisses that were spreading up her legs were more like Owen was making love to her. While this is not what she wanted, she was already so wet inside; she could do nothing but moan in passion.

As his lips tasted Caroline's legs and worked up toward her naked pussy, his hands spread up to her butt and began to sensuously massage her cheeks. Now Caroline's body was responding. Her mind told her to get out of bed and stop it, but when she moved, some of the sheet came off. Even though she didn't have to be, Caroline was naked under that sheet.

Just then, she felt Owen crawling on his hands and knees up to her. Caroline opened her thighs so he could penetrate her. She did feel her pussy spread open, but it was Owen's fingers parting the slit and caressing her clit and the rim of her vagina. When his index finger slid up inside her, Caroline moaned loudly and brought a leg up which pushed the sheet off almost to her shoulders.

Caroline felt Owen's loving hands on her sides moving up to her shoulders. He slowly peeled the sheet off of her shoulder and then over her head. When Caroline turned her face to meet his, she was frightened and aroused all at once. But then he kissed her. That kiss changed everything as Caroline's heart melted and she wanted him inside her at the same time.

Caroline rolled over and pulled Owen into her arms kissing him eagerly. Owen pushed her legs.

"I want to fuck you so bad Caroline."

"Yes darling, I want to have your baby."

She spread her thighs to take him inside her. Now, she wanted it to be his baby as though she had forgotten all about her husband. She didn't have to wait long. Owen found her wet opening with his hard cock and slid inside of her, easily filling every inch of her pussy.

Owen buried his face in her small breasts, kissing and sucking as Caroline wept with emotion and passion and fucked back up to his steady thrusts inside her.

Owen began to fuck Caroline fast and hard pushing up to look down on her gorgeous face and body as she was giving everything to him. He saw his wet cock slide out of her tiny pussy hole and drive back in. Caroline was gasping and thrusting fucking him as much as he was fucking her. "I'm going to cum, Caroline," he moaned, and she only went wilder, waiting to take his sperm.

Owen collapsed on her and drove his cock into her again and again and again. Just then his balls constricted and huge streams of cum filled Caroline's insides. Caroline felt the hot cum filling her up and she orgasmed too holding on to Owen's neck and moaning,

"Oh yes, oh yes, oh yes."

When it was over, Owen and Caroline kissed and whispered how amazing that was. Over at Owen's home, Richard and Angela were kissing softly as his cum spilled inside her. There would be much to sort out, but the universe had left four very satisfied lovers in each other's arms. The rest was all just details.

14 COMMUNITY THEATER

Bob had a lot to offer the community theatre because he had served on boards before. He was dedicated to getting the Mossberry Community Theatre into shape. After a couple of years with some smart management, and some savvy play selection, they started selling tickets. In fact, by the beginning of the third year, season tickets to the Mossberry Community Theatre were sold out. That made Bob a bona fide hero of the local arts community. This wasn't a bad job for an introverted accountant.

One of Bob's tasks was to meet with local civic leaders to get feedback on the theatre and to solicit donations. They got more of their budget from those efforts than from selling tickets. The meetings were held in a conference room of one of churches in town.

The church had a campus that was bigger than the college, and they had over 20,000 members from all around the state. Bob liked using their very upscale conference room.

The leaders who came to the May meeting included local presidents and pastors of churches and other representatives of civic organizations and businesses that patronized the arts. Bob was skilled at romancing big shots and coaxing donations from them in exchange for a chance to be in a crowd scene in a play and free front row tickets to a popular performance.

The church provided a young woman to keep minutes, serve refreshments and take care of any other secretarial needs. Her name was Lisa and she did a great job. She was also quite pretty which didn't hurt with the older guys who liked the eye candy. Bob thought it was a little twisted that they tried to stare at her legs in her cute short skirt, but if it got more donations and they were only looking, no harm done.

As the meeting wrapped up, Lisa stayed around to help clean up and to make sure everything was documented. It was very important that the details of any donations were noted particularly. Lisa and Bob went over her notes at the big table to finalize all of that. Lisa's day job was as a secretary so her clerical skills were strong. Bob was impressed with Lisa. She looked like a teenager, but she was 21 and did a lot of work for the church as well as keeping up with her own job.

"It must be so exciting to be involved with theatre."

"Yes, this is a job I can do for the company since I can't act."

Bob laughed well naturedly.

"And I get free tickets and I can sit in on the rehearsals and put my two cents in every so often. My wife and kids love the shows and knowing the actors by name too."

"Oh, I would love to see a rehearsal sometime."

She bent over to put away the coffee pots under the cabinet. Her short skirt rode up. Bob had to notice how sexy her legs looked. He was able to see a glimpse of her panties and that was a nice private peek he could save in his mind for later. Lisa walked over to the table where Bob was standing up and tilted her head flirtatiously while flipping her hair.

"Do you think I would make a good actress?"

She giggled and then she put her hand on the back of his on the table. It was clearly a flirt. Bob smiled back at the pretty girl admiring her pretty blond hair that came to just below her chin.

"I am sure you would do well at anything you try Lisa

"I would love any help you could give me to get started being an actress. That would be so exciting and you are so sweet."

She kissed him on the cheek. Bob knew that was inappropriate but the place was empty and it was just a kiss. He felt Lisa's hand move from his own to his pants. She skilfully rubbed up and down on the front of his pants finding his penis inside. It did not take long before Bob got an erection.

"I want to give you my phone number and..."

Lisa unzipped Bob's pants. Bob felt light-headed. He was not used to a gorgeous young woman being so forward with him. Bob was paralysed. He knew he should stop, but his hard-on was not having that. Bob felt like he was watching it happen to him as Lisa pushed her hand inside his pants, pulled his underwear aside and grasped his very hard cock pulling it out of his fly.

"Oh God, Lisa, this is so wrong."

Lisa stroked his hard cock up and down making Bob moan and thrust his hips into her hand.

"Do you think I am sexy, Mr. Mullins?" she whispered as he rubbed her chest against his.

"Oh yes Lisa, you are amazing."

That was enough encouragement for her. She slid down his body to her knees with her face right in front of his hard cock. Before Bob could gather his wits, the pretty young woman slid his cock past her full and round lips and began to suck it expertly. As guilty as he felt, he could not help feeling very turned on as she licked his balls and then took his hard shaft in her mouth again.

He wanted to go to the floor with that gorgeous secretary and fuck her brains out. But he was too far gone. Suddenly he felt his orgasm gathering.

"Oh God Lisa, I am going to cum in your

mouth."

That only made Lisa more aggressive, moving her mouth back and forth so his wet cock fucked in and out of her lips rapidly. When he shot, she slid the head to the middle of her mouth and used her tongue on the underside to coax the sperm out of his penis. His cum shot into her mouth and she swallowed it spurt by spurt.

Lisa promised Bob that their moment would remain a secret. She helped him clean up and they moved to the door of the conference room. But just before he closed the door, she leaned up and kissed his lips deeply. Then she whispered, "I want to come to these meetings all the time, Mr. Mullins." Bob felt certain he could and would make that happen.

The Performers

Bob got to the theatre a little late because of his time with Lisa. He wanted to have a little time with the troupe leaders to review the notes from the meeting. On stage, an acting class was doing exercises. Leo, the primary director, was working with two actresses on an acting exercise. Bob settled into a seat to watch this part of the preparation process.

"No, no girls, I need more intensity from you! You are angry because Amy, your husband Josh has been cheating with Chelsea." Leo said with frustration. "Listen, work on this in rehearsal room seven with Mr. Rutgers and we will continue later in the hour."

Amy and Chelsea left the stage and Mr. Rutgers appeared from the wings to go to the rehearsal room with the girls. Mr. Rutgers also did some directing and he was part of the props or stage crew for almost every play they did. He knew what Leo was after. The theatre was housed in an old house and they had converted all of the lower sections to theatre space. The second floor had smaller spaces were used for rehearsal or small presentations and then the old bedrooms were used for offices or for places where two or three performers could work out glitches in a scene like the two girls were doing.

Amy was a petite red haired girl with lots of freckles. She had almost a boyish figure with just a hint of breasts inside of her shirt. She wore cut offs, a sleeveless shirt and over that she wore long sleeved work open with the ends tied around her middle. Chelsea was much more voluptuous. While not fat, she was round in every place. She wore a cute white skirt that showed off her very round thighs nicely. Her top cut off just below her large and sexy breasts but it gave her plenty of comfort for acting class.

"Ok girls, let's just talk through the scene from your scripts first."

As the girls read their parts, they stood in the middle of the room and spoke their lines to each other in front of the couches that were kept in there. Chelsea and Amy had been good friends since high school so it was hard for them to pretend to be mad at each other.

"Ok that was good," Mr. Rutgers coached them. "Now perform it and give me lots of passion."

Amy and Chelsea knew their lines so they put down their scripts and used every ounce of acting skill they had to be furious with each other. But Mr. Rutgers was not satisfied. "Girls I want to put you on that stage out there exploding with passion for this scene. You need to orgasm anger here."

"Mr. Rutgers," Chelsea said respectfully. "That term is hard to figure out when we are supposed to be mad. I think it is because when I think of passion, I think, you know, of the sexual kind." She finished.

"Ok let's work from that starting place as an exercise. Follow my directions to the letter. Ready and go," Mr. Rutgers said. "Amy, grab Chelsea by the arms, look at her in the eyes and think to her, 'I want to fuck you,'" he ordered.

"Oh my God, Mr. Rutgers!" Amy gasped. "We are not lesbians at all!"

"Then you will have to act! Now convince me! Grab her now Amy."

Amy sunk her teeth into the role. She roughly grabbed her old friend by the arms and squeezed her flesh in her in fingers. "Oh!" Chelsea gasped at being so roughly handled. The look in Amy's eyes was hungry and rough.

"I want to fuck you." Amy said in a low growl.

"Improve girls, go with it," Mr. Rutgers coached watching closely. "Amy, dominate Chelsea. Chelsea, you are submissive," He said in a low tone so as not to break the creative flow of the performers.

"Oh yes, mistress, take me." Chelsea moaned throwing her head back. Amy pulled Chelsea to her demandingly and fell on her neck sucking it and biting her ears. The motions were improved acting, but more and more the girls became aroused by each other.

"Oh God Amy, yes," Chelsea moaned but now she was not acting. She fell back on to the couch and pulled Amy on top of her.

"That's good girls, passion," Mr. Rutgers encouraged them, but he also knew that this had stopped being acting. He noticed he had a hard on watching the two actress friends. Amy fell on top of Chelsea and shoved a hand under her top, which contacted her naked breast. Roughly, Amy pulled Chelsea's top down so her gorgeous left tit came out, showing the pink, very round and hard nipple.

Amy sat up to look at Chelsea's breast when Chelsea became aggressive. She reached out and yanked down on Amy's top tearing it. Her fingers hooked in Amy's bra and pulled it down showing her smaller tits to her new lover and to Mr. Rutgers. By this time, Mr. Rutgers was so stirred up by what was going on that he had unzipped his pants, pulled out his hard cock, and started masturbating watching the girls.

The girls crawled all over each other on

that couch - touching, feeling and kissing. Soon Amy had pulled Chelsea's skirt up and worked her panties down her thighs so she could get to her sexy pussy. Mr. Rutgers was on his feet and coming closer, pulling on his rock hard cock the whole time. As he looked down, he saw Amy's fingers spread Chelsea's pussy lips to reveal her tiny clit and that gorgeous pink slit.

Chelsea was pulling on Amy's pants so they worked down her butt revealing her slender ass cheeks and her sexy butt crack. Mr. Rutgers got involved pulling Amy's pants further down and when he stood up, Chelsea had pushed her fingers into Amy's cunt and was stroking her clit. Both girls were moaning as their fingers began to explore inside those wet vaginas.

Suddenly Mr. Rutgers peaked watching the girls kissing, sucking and fingering each other and his cum shot out of his cock and landed all over the sexy couple. The girls felt his spray of cum and did not look up from each other. But he had no sooner shot on them when the speaker for the theatre spoke up.

"Mr. Rutgers, to the stage please?"

The acting coach quickly pushed his cock back in his shorts and fixed himself the best he could. He rushed out to the main stage of the theatre. Leo the head director of the community theatre was working with two more actors. He looked up at his associate and asked him...

"Well Max, did the girls find their passion for that scene?"

"They really did, Leo," Mr. Rutgers answered. "They really did.

The Storm

Bob enjoyed Saturday lunch with his beautiful wife Anne, and Steven and Sydney, the twins. The episode with Lisa had faded. He saw Lisa at the theatre often and the heat between them was still strong. But she knew as he did that they could not have a heated affair in that setting. That would have to wait for privacy and the right time.

Since Bob became involved with the Mossbery Community Theater, Anne had gotten used to him running down to the playhouse to check on things. She and the kids were proud of how respected he was for his work with the theatre and they supported it entirely. As Bob was changing clothes to head to the theatre, his cell phone rang. He looked at the caller ID and it was his very good friend David. He had known David for decades and his daughter Laura had a role in a production that was in rehearsals, Little Women.

"What's up David?" he answered.

"Bob, are you going to rehearsal tonight?" David asked. When David assured him he would be there, David asked for a favor. "It is going to be stormy tonight and I don't like Laura driving. I am out of town so I cannot take her home. Her friend Samantha will drop her off at the theatre but if you could make sure Laura gets home safe, I would owe you big time."

"No debt needed my friend." Bob said cheerfully. "You know I love Laura to pieces. I will make sure she gets home safe and sound."

Everybody in the community had been a bit protective of Laura. She was a gorgeous girl with a pure and sweet manner about her that could melt the heart of any living thing. But Laura had gotten through a tough childhood. Around the age of 11, she contracted a spinal disease that was often fatal. It was touch and go for many years. But through a lot of tears, tender loving care, many medical interventions and some serious determination on Laura's part, she fought back to almost full functionality. She still had to do physical therapy and she wore brace on her right leg. She walked with a very slight limp but in every other way, Laura was a winner.

Laura was an amazing young woman. At 19, her achievements were phenomenal. She was a straight "A" student, on every committee at school and church and had been involved in dozens of civic and mission projects. Laura was loved by all. It didn't hurt that except for the small limp, Laura was stunningly beautiful.

When Bob got to the rehearsal, it was already getting stormy outside. He sat in the audience seats and enjoyed the mechanics of theatre rehearsal. His eyes rested on Laura mostly, perhaps because he had the responsibility to get her home. Finally, the director, Leo, adjourned the rehearsal so everyone could get home safely.

Laura cheerfully found Bob after she gathered her things. "Thanks for taking me home Mr. Mullins."

Bob and Laura chattered about the play and the theatre all the way home. She was a delightful girl to talk to. It was pitch black when he pulled up in her driveway and she had to walk around to the side door to go in. As she opened the car door, there was a sudden loud noise like a door being slammed shut and it seemed like a figure was moving in the shadows. Laura looked very nervous.

"Let me walk you to the door."

The young woman seemed very relieved by his offer. It was dark around the sides of the house but Laura had her key ready. When she opened the door, it was pitch black inside. Then there was another slam that perhaps could have been coming from somewhere nearby where a loose screen door was being slammed by the wind. Laura jumped and grabbed Bob's hand.

"Please come in with me to make sure the house is safe."

As Bob and Laura checked out the house, her nervousness only subsided a little. Just then, the power went out and the storm intensified. When the living room went dark, Bob felt the young woman grasp his chest and hold him. He comforted her by saying that it was only a power outage.

Laura found some candles and before

long, they had the living room lit with the warm glow of 7 big candles that were burning safely.

"I am a little scared, Mr. Mullins."

Bob did not feel he could leave her alone there just yet. Just then, her phone rang. "Oh hi Daddy. No, Mr. Mullins is still here. Daddy wants to talk to you."

Bob took the phone.

"Would you mind staying the night there? Laura can fix up a place on the couch for you."

Bob assured David he would not abandon his precious daughter. Quickly he called his wife Anne at home. He was relieved to hear they were safe and riding out the storm.

"Of course Bob. Staying with her is the right thing to do. I don't want you driving in this storm anyway. See you in the morning, darling."

Laura was delighted and relieved that Bob was staying. Soon they were settled in the living room talking and joking to make the time pass.

"I can get you some wine if you want."

Bob agreed that would calm his nerves so she found a bottle of merlot that was very good. When Bob offered her a sip, she giggled because she had not had wine before. Soon she had sipped so much that she had to get her own glass. "This is an adventure. Trying new things."

After the talking and enjoying wine had been going on a while, both Bob and Laura got very relaxed. He lay back on the couch and she got a big blanket and snuggled up next to him.

"Mmmm," she said softly. "You cuddle almost as good as my daddy."

He found that idea a little odd because he did not see himself in that role. He was just being a good friend. The longer they snuggled, the more affectionate she became. Suddenly Bob felt a little kiss in his jaw.

"You are so brave to protect me."

Bob looked into her gorgeous eyes that seemed to draw him in. Then without thinking, he went with the moment and softly kissed her lips. That "what are you doing?" thought came to Bob as he kissed Laura but she seemed to fall under the spell of the intimacy of the moment and kissed him back. As much as he fought the desire inside him, he felt the rise of his erection just under the body of the pretty girl who was lying on him.

Laura was a virgin. She knew boys wanted her, but her handicap and strong reputation with her family and church assured she would not be hit on by guys who wanted to take her virginity. But as she kissed Mr. Mullins, she felt his hard-on under her and got excited by it. She looked at him and softly whispered, "I feel it."

"I am sorry, Laura." He said reflecting his embarrassment.

"Is that because of me?" She said curiously. "I have never made anyone get like that."

"Well it happens to a male at times. But the wine, the closeness and the kissing helped. And you are a beautiful girl," Bob said sincerely.

"I am kinda excited Mr. Mullins," Laura whispered. "Is that ok?" Bob was a little nervous holding the beautiful 19 year old in his arms as his hard on pressed against her tummy. But he assured her that it was fine and she was safe. "Do you think I can see it?" she asked suddenly. Bob was stunned at her question. "Please don't be mad and it will always be our secret," she assured him.

With some reluctance and nervousness, he agreed to it. Laura rolled over to lie side by side with him on the big couch and then Bob unzipped his pants. In the soft candlelight, he saw her eyes grow wide when he took out his hard cock and let her gaze at it. It was clear that Laura was very turned on. Without even asking, she put her fingers on it and began to caress the tip and explore the shaft and his balls.

Staring at his hard cock, Laura was mesmerized. She said softly, "Is this hard because you are turned on by me, Mr. Mullins?" Bob had lost track of the responsible adult he was supposed to be and simply responded that he was. When he said that, Laura laid back and pulled him to her. "I am so turned on too," She moaned kissing him. "I want you to have sex with me. Take my virginity."

The storm was calming down as intensity heated up on that couch. Tenderly Bob took his time removing Laura's blouse and bra. Her breasts were gorgeous. They were full and round. The nipples were pointy and became more pronounced when Bob leaned in and kissed them. "Oh God, Mr. Mullins," she moaned, "Suck my breasts, I want to know how that feels."

The beautiful girl went wild when Bob slipped her right nipple into his mouth and sucked it. By now, his body was going crazy wanting to fuck this sweet innocent and very sexy girl. Bob leaned over and pushed his pants down and off. She helped him out of his shirt and began to caress his naked torso when she saw his muscles. That was all it took to let any last objections die. Bob kissed Laura sweetly with a long, sexy wet kiss as he pulled up her skirt. Laura helped him by starting to wiggle her panties down.

Bob pushed them down the rest of the way and then laid her on the couch so she could spread her legs to be fucked, and finally forget about being a virgin. He was tender with her to protect the brace on her lower leg but even mild twinges of pain that she got from it could not overpower the fire in her pussy as it yearned to feel the sensation of being penetrated.

Lying on the lovely girl, Bob reached down and guided the tip of his cock to the opening of her wet vagina. "Don't be scared," he assured her, "I will be gentle."

"I want this so bad Mr. Mullins," she whispered, kissing his neck. The feel of the rim of her wet hole pulling on the tip of his cock was amazing. Pressing to go in, Bob felt Laura gasp and push up, moaning at the pain and the pleasure of becoming a woman. Just then, the tip of Bob's cock pushed inside of her tight virgin cunt. Laura thrust her naked tits into his chest and kissed him hungrily. "Tell me what you are going to do to me," she said lustfully.

"I am fucking you." Bob said sucking her neck and pressing. Inch by inch, Bob's big hard cock stretched Laura's insides.

"Oh God Yes!" she moaned, pushing back to get more of him inside her. At about half penetration, Bob began to fuck the beautiful actress. His powerful thrusts took him deeper and deeper until he was able to get all of his hard-on inside her.

"Fuck me!" she said, turned on by being a dirty girl instead of the perfect princess for once. Bob reached around, grabbed the soft flesh of Laura's sweet ass cheeks, and squeezed them. Pulling her cunt to him, he started fucking into her again and again and again and again and again. She was a wild girl under him, arching up and moaning until suddenly spasms seemed to take her over as she had the most powerful orgasm of her life.

Just as quickly, Bob's climax hit him. He pushed up on his hands looking down to see all but the base of his cock disappeared inside of Laura's pussy hole. Without hesitation, he let his orgasm strike and he began to pump stream after hot stream of cum inside of her tight womb.

As the orgasms subsided, Bob laid on the young girl. They kissed and they dozed off with him still inside her. When he woke up with the beautiful young girl naked on the couch with him, he felt grief, remorse and happiness. She woke up and kissed him and whispered, "I love you" to him. While it was wrong he fucked the community theatre princess and cherished daughter of one of his best friends, Bob could not help but say it back to her because it was the truth when he said to her, "Laura, I love you too."

AUTHOR'S NOTE

Readers: I want to expand a few of the stories to see where the characters can be explored further. If there are any of the stories that you would like to read more about again, I'd love to hear from you!

Visit my blog at
http://www.stefanmckinnis.com

Join my newsletter for free exclusive previews
http://www.stefanmckinnis.com/in

Follow me on Twitter at
http://www.twitter.com/stefanmckinnis

Like my page on Facebook at
http://www.facebook.com/stefanmckinnis

Discover my books at major ebook retailers everywhere.